Naughty Indian Affairs

Sonny Singh Kalar

www.masalabooks.com   masalabooks@yahoo.com

Grosvenor House
Publishing Limited

This book is published by
Grosvenor House Publishing Ltd
28-30 High Street, Guildford, Surrey, GU1 3HY.
www.grosvenorhousepublishing.co.uk

**All the characters in this book are fictitious, and any resemblance to
actual persons, living or dead, is purely coincidental.**

A CIP record for this book
is available from the British Library

ISBN 978-1-906210-90-8

Special love for -
Meena, Roops, Jasmin and Danni.
May God bless you in everything you do!

A note from the Author...

<u>'Vita sine libris mors est'</u>   <u>- Life without books is death</u>

*Your life is waiting for you to unleash
your spirit and magic on it...
You are the creator of your own destiny.
What you want out of life, how you feel about
those around you, it all stems from believing who
you are and what you aspire to achieve in your kingdom.
Motivate, inspire and take others with you on
your whirlwind journey wherever and whatever
your destination is; it is the excitement of your
desire and vision that is all important.
It is imperative that you remain positive, happy and
forward thinking in all facets of your journey through life
and you will attract only good things to you, this is a firm
tenet of the law of attraction. Above all, you must believe
in your dreams and stir your heart with visions of grandeur
and success; only then will you guarantee that positive
energies will find a path to you. Remember that regrets
weigh you down like an anvil. You have one life so make
the most of it, be happy, healthy and adventurous.*

<u>'Fortitudine Vincimus'</u>   <u>By endurance we conquer</u>

'ROCKING SINGH'S COFFEE SHOP'

'THE MASALA BEER FACTORY'

Contents

CHAPTER 1

—∞—

Predatory lust

3 Months ago – 5th May 2007

'A sexy Indian girl with pure filthy lust on her mind is the ticket to nirvana most guys dream about, and Punjabi girls simply do not come any hotter, raunchier and as sexually ravishing as Raj Dhaliwal.'

Raj leaned over the kitchen table top to get as close to him as possible, her target of lust, a man she has been eyeing up for what seemed like an eternity. She was within adequate pouncing range, standing on her toes as she stretched the contours of her voluptuous body across the counter towards Manjit as he spoke on his phone, completely incognizant to the sexy predator eyeing up her quarry beside him.

She had seen and been with many men over her 32 years but she had never wanted someone as much and painfully as she desired her Asian stud who dangled in front of her like a ripe and juicy carrot. Her black skirt hitched up and slightly revealing the sexiest and most curvaceous legs this side of town. The endless contours of her body lending a certain 'masala' to her aura. Her size ten frame, beautiful green eyes and not to mention radiant fair skinned appearance, the perfect aphrodisiac for any red blooded male.

Her earlier call to Sehmbi's Estate Agents in Hounslow, where he was employed as a shrewd operating estate agent had worked like a treat. She had requested a viewing of an unoccupied three bedroom detached house that she had seen advertised in Cromwell Road. It was exclusively advertised by Sehmbi's Estate Agency and was the perfect combination to snare her man she had thought.

She had planned it meticulously calling up and leaving her name as Ms Kandhola, suggesting that she was interested in viewing properties that very day, registering her details and then mentioning that she wanted Manjit to attend, as his name was given to her by a business associate. Well this painstaking planning had paid off when Manjit had arrived exactly on the nose, 10am sharp, pulling up in his black BMW X5. He walked up smoothly to the front door flicking his wrist up and checking the time. He had looked around before opening the door and entering the house. Raj had remained in her car and at a safe distance observing Manjit as he arrived at the venue, only approaching the front door when he was safely inside awaiting his potential house buyer.

She stood outside composing herself, mumbling words of self reassurance and edification as the sting of the morning sun tempered by a feisty breeze swept across her face. The lush garden bush beside her was gently swaying and caressing the flowers adorning the verdant lawn. The blooming daffodils juxtaposed by fragrant roses. The fresh smell of summer continued licking the air surrounding her. She rang the bell, nervous and peppered with knee shaking trepidation for what she had yearned for.

'What you doing here?' he asked raising his eyebrow upon opening the door. His mere hunky presence sending waves of ecstasy shuttling around her nerve jangled body. However, his initial surprise and confusion was soon dissipated when Raj had explained that she had needed to speak with him about an urgent matter, and that this had been the only conceivable way in which to do this.

They then went inside after exchanging conversational pleasantries on the doorstep walking through to the kitchen area. Suddenly his mobile phone rang as they both stood opposite each other across the kitchen table top.

The call had deftly shattered the momentum that Raj was building up, her master plan being put on hold for a few more agonising seconds.

Manjit turned around facing away from her, and negotiated into the phone with one of his landlord clients with agency related work. Meanwhile Raj leaned forward onto the flat surfaced counter and waited there patiently. She did not speak, but instead studied his every twitch like a meer cat suffering from incurable insomnia. She sized him up, he was the whole package, at 5ft 10 tall, strong and muscular. His broad, manly shoulders making her weak at the knees, his toned and athletic appearance was too much to resist. She had wanted him for an eternity and here he was literally on a plate for her a mere kiss away from full on physical action in bed with her much lusted after fantasy man.

He lowered the phone from his ear and put it back into his jacket pocket before turning to face her, still looking confused as to why she had not left her real name and what was so urgent that she couldn't have just phoned him or popped into his office. They stared at one another for a moment; no words were exchanged just physical electricity between them. It was tangible and undeniable to both of them. The sort of feeling you get when you are about to do something risky and naughty but know that the feeling of orgasmic pleasure that you are about to feel is worth the thrill and rush.

Her face gently resting on her hands, elbows on the counter and gazing up at her prey.

Her lips were pouting, the thick red texture of her lipstick luring him into this treacherous honey trap; a move that he may regret for as long as he lived.

She reached out and began stroking his arm as he leaned forward resting it on the counter. Her soft touch and incontestable intent was turning him on. He had similarly held a torch for her since the time they had known each other. She was beautiful, a stunning Indian girl, the sort that he would dream about caressing, holding and making desperate love to.

Raj, was determined and began running her fingers in between the gap in the bottom of his shirt sleeve, gently playing with his arm hair. She twirled the strands of hair around her fingers and manoeuvred her body subtly from around the kitchen top counter. There was sexual tension, urgency in the air between them, she could feel the waves of sexy chemicals swimming through her body, the first date butterflies making her stomach somersault, the anticipation and excitement that she was about to fulfil her wildest of wild fantasies was all too much; the juices flowed freely and with abundant pleasure.

She felt like melting into him as he pulled her close to him with one quick jerking motion. He too knew how badly they both wanted this to happen. It was wrong but even at this stage, they were past the point of no return; it was just a matter of delicate seconds before the encounter was to become physical, sweaty and unforgettable.

He whispered 'do you really want this?' His hot and heavy breath now felt on her soft fair skinned cheek. His breathing becoming heavier from the surreptitious encounter that he had found himself in and the passionate sexual urges inching him on to fulfil his caveman quest, the tension and desire to take her right there and then on the table top in unrelenting, all consuming sexual frustration, the pressure was feverish and electric. Her lasciviousness was continuing to warm his heart, and stir his nether regions in equal measure.

Raj took a hold of the lapels of his suit jacket and tugged him gently towards her quaking body 'I can't live my life with just one guy. I need to allow myself to stray just once. I am prepared to have that one affair with you. Just one time of raunchy sex with you. She blushed suggestively, her face moved closer to his as she spoke, severely testing his will power and mettle in this cooking furnace. 'I just want to feel lusted over by someone like you, just one time, one mad time, like now…'

Manjit placed his hands tenderly on the sides of her face 'are you sure, because once we cross this line then things will never be the same again, especially in our circles…?'

His words carrying an air of caution with the caveat to come to their senses before the matter spiralled into a murky lust fuelled abyss, the point of no return. 'I have never wanted anything more in my whole…'

He grabbed her hair tightly around the back of her head, clutching her tresses with a hardened passion. He thrust his manly lips onto her quivering red lipstick, hard and passionately. The soft fair skin of her face touching his scrubbed clean cut face as they embraced passionately. He had to have her right there and then, he could resist no more. He pushed her back a few steps as she crashed into the side of the kitchen table, he quickly ran his other hand viciously across the kitchen table knocking off the condiments and scattering them across the room, the salt and pepper pots clattering to the floor around their feet. She felt a sudden weakness in her legs as they buckled in the throes of illicit passion.

He rolled his head around hers as they embraced sensually; both of them exploring each others bodies with roaming hands, there were no boundaries as this went on for a few minutes. Any apprehension at that moment went crash landing, plummeting to the dirt quicker than the thrusting of Norman Bates knife in the shower scene. The iron skillet of marital trust disappearing in a puff of smoke as their mouths remained glued together passionately.

He then gently lifted Raj onto the kitchen table and laid her back as he continued passionately kissing her. He worked his lips around her neck for several moments. She could do nothing more but lie back, completely at his mercy, her legs wrapped tightly around his waist, squeezing as hard as she could and enjoying every kiss, every hot breath and every touch like she was a virginal lover. She drew him in closer and closer, it was as though their bodies were one, entwined in pleasure.

They both revelled in the throes of this illicit, dangerous affair. Her body throbbed, her heart thumped like a piston, she had never been taken like this before, ever. Her husband was the last person on her mind, his sexual technique was no comparison to this burning stud lavishing over her right now in this moment of extra marital lust. This cuckold *(name of a female who cheats on her husband – derived from the female cuckoo bird who lays its eggs in another female's nest therefore freeing themselves from nurturing the eggs to hatching)* was revelling in the moment, her eyes rolling back in ecstasy.

He then scooped her up in his manly arms, both of them with clothes unbuckled, then proceeded upstairs into the furnished bedroom, kicking open the door as he gently threw Raj onto her back before fully removing his clothes. Raj followed suit and tossed her clothes across the room. He simply could not resist the urges screaming from his pulsating body any longer.

She had a body that would drive any red blooded man crazy. Her glowing and gorgeous skin, large breasts, long and curvy legs, silky black hair with streaks of brown running throughout, and the green eyes that melted the staunchest of happily married men. This would be the case when they were staring up in eager anticipation from underneath her, as he squeezed her hair in his manly grip with furious passion, moments away from stoking her fire with adulterous aplomb. Her coy little smile was swathed in self indulgent vigour as she threw her head back, her eyes twinkling and rolling back like a slot machine.

She needed this after years of perfunctory sex with her husband. She had been shuffling along aimlessly in a predictable and humdrum lifestyle. Despite being married for 3 years, this was her single most satisfying experience to date. She had sometimes told work colleagues that she would count up to 20 seconds in her head from the moment her husband mounted her to the moment he exploded, and nigh on every time on precisely the count to 20 the deed was executed with precision, before he would slope off into a satisfying slumber next to her. She would often confess that he had the sex appeal of a wet paper bag and stimulated her as much as a warty and gangrened nipple.

He continued to kiss her hard and indulged in the next few minutes of the most desirable pleasure he had ever experienced, the thrill of the chase, the naughtiness of the affair, his wife but a distant memory. She had never given him a feeling like this, an uncontrolled feeling of ecstasy, his loins burning with anticipation. Nothing could have beaten the sheer excitement and danger that was rapidly filling the room.

Manjit had always loved Asian girls, the way they held themselves, the way they could dress up in traditional suits and look stunning were part of the alluring factors that brought him to this conclusion. The word monogamy buried under the swathes of sexual tension filling every crevice of the room as their hot, sweaty, naked and pulsating bodies writhed around from position to position with expert and lustful aplomb. His nubile and agile body entwined with hers as though they were one.

He loved the fact that Raj knew how to express herself in between the sheets, especially as he looked down at her as she writhed her body snake like before his very eyes. He kissed up and down her sexy legs; both of them now drizzled in sweat. He held her tightly in his arms as they both rocked to pleasure. A few minutes later it was done, as they jointly screamed in ecstasy, both of them satisfied equally. The moment was firmly sealed in the annals of history. This was the point of no return, they had fulfilled their darkest fantasy after several months of knife edge flirting in their meetings and encounters with one another.

Manjit climbed off her while Raj propped herself up by her elbows on the tempur bed mattress sinking in a few inches as she did so. They had flirted with the tempestuous flames of passion, and had both been sucked into the burning pyres.

She satisfyingly purred 'god I have needed that for ages, tell me your wife has never had sex with you like that big boy?' He was immensely and deeply satisfied as he fell on the bed on his back, panting and stroking his chest 'baby where have you been hiding all this time, that was...'

She leaned on top of him and kissed his lips tenderly, teasingly moving her face away biting his bottom lip with dirty passion as she did so. He was lapping up every drop of this illicit affair, and then the guilt set in. The physical craving for her sexy body was now slowly being replaced with an over whelming feeling of self loathing and disgust. He had cheated on his wife – Kully, for the first time in their relationship. He started to dress himself, his gut twisting with each button he twisted in his shirt with the thought of his deceit, his surreptitious actions defiling his normally steadfast and monogamous stance on extra marital relations.

Raj, meanwhile manoeuvred herself off the bed and sauntered sexily over to the bathroom. Manjit could not resist looking at her pert brown bum as she closed the door behind her, the perfect wobble and succulent softness that almost made him forget those feelings of guilt for a second.

It has been recorded statistically that the reason why a large percentage of men and women cheated was because they wanted sex more frequently and others simply an injection of sexual variety. The cold and shocking reality is that Manjit is one of a clutch of married men who find the urge, the incessant need to stray at least once during their marriage as compiled in one of a myriad of statistics surveyed around the globe. They say that half of men and half of women in any form of relationship have cheated at some point in their lives. Both of these troopers had played their dutiful part in upholding such statistics in the aftermath of their romp.

However, Manjit had no excuse as he had a healthy sex life with Kully, and she was ordinarily a willing participant in between the sheets.

He had survived the myriad peaks and prairies of married life with his loving wife, which made matters worse.

This smacked of pure animal lust, nothing more and nothing less. The snap and thrill of the affair, the thrust of power of taking another man's wife in his arms in this dark and seductive fling were contributing factors for his thirst to be sexually entangled in this web of treachery. Some things it appeared were standard in life, for example, when someone yawns, you yawn, when someone is sick it makes you feel sick, when someone offers you free no strings attached sex, you indulge in free no strings attached sex.

He had wanted a piece of her body for some time now and in his head he had nailed his darkest fantasy by laying her today, although the set up was instigated by

Raj, to whom he was most grateful. Whilst he slipped into his jacket and straightened his tie in the mirror, she emerged from the bathroom – fresh faced and beautiful, her legs looking just as teasingly appealing as a few minutes ago.

He walked over to her and caressed her cheeks with both hands 'well my darling that was beacoup' He said whilst kissing her on the lips. 'I must dash, you okay?'

'Yeah, I am now, I feel like partying.' she purred back, her rosy cheeks and pouting lips tempting Manjit into round two. However, he relented against pinning her back on the bed and smiled before turning to walk out of the bedroom scooping his BMW car keys up from within his jacket pocket and twirling them in his fingers.

'Hey.' she tugged him back by his arm. He stopped and surveyed her face. Was something wrong? He was about to find out.

He knew that she found him irresistible but surely she would understand that he had appointments and clients to attend to rather than spend the entire day fornicating in this carefree and incautious manner.

'When are we going to do this again?' she asked, a pleading tone permeating her words.

Manjit smiled 'I thought you said it was just going to be the one time.' He teased her playfully 'don't worry leave it to me, maybe tomorrow if I can get things sorted at work...but hey we have to be careful. Raj screwed her eyes up at him 'what do you mean we have to be careful, don't treat me like a child.' The swipe about *being the one time* the underlying cause of her miffed response.

Manjit was a little taken aback by her comment and quickly sought to reassure her and justify his remark 'no, all I am saying is that with the relationships we have – it is all too easy to slip up with the odd comment or whatever.'

Raj rolled her eyes and peered out of the window with her arms folded, a clear sign of her indignation towards him at this precise moment, despite the euphoric emotions and love they had shared only moments before.

'We just have to be careful, I mean me equally, that is all, don't get into a strop over what I said, okay.'

Manjit looked at his watch again 'I have to go or they will be sending out the blood hounds searching for me, ciao.'

He leant forward to kiss her on the cheek and she allowed him to do so albeit with a tinge of reluctance.

He turned his back and as he did, she quickly wiped the wet saliva from his kiss off her cheek with a forceful angry swipe downwards. Manjit meanwhile had left the room and was waiting outside the house for her, Raj joined him several seconds later, and they both got into their respective cars and went their separate ways. Manjit drove off down the road heading to his next appointment, the soothing sounds of Juggy D playing out from his speakers, a feeling of utter satisfaction and contentment radiating throughout his body, electricity akin to that you get when you have sex for the first time.

The fact that she had chosen him as the one guy she would go over the side with was edifying and flattering for him as he recalled their passionate embrace repeatedly in his mind. His sexual urge in taking his mistress in his arms, making his lover look deep into his eyes in total ecstasy and unfulfilled lust begging and imploring him to take her. It was all about the power, control and physical domination (he cranked up the music to volume ten).

He sped down the road physically and emotionally satisfied and without an obvious care in the world, when all of a sudden the guilt and treachery smacked him straight between the eyes, hit him with full unrestrained force. It was the sudden paroxysm of betrayal lurching up and throttling his throat as he quickly pulled over to the side of the road. His gut was churning around with thoughts of his duplicity and hurtful actions. The last thing that he wanted to come out of this affair was a tear strained divorce break up. He had simply not signed up for that as the reality and ramifications of the situation sledge hammered into his chest repeatedly.

He rested his spinning head on the steering wheel as the knot in his stomach tightened, the rucksack of guilt wearing him down. Visions of his wife Kully, beautiful and heart warming came into his head. She was a lady with a strong resolute nerve entwined with delicate manners and a lost innocence and above all she loved him, doted on his every action or word. Yet here he was a cheater. What had compelled him to cheat? His mind asking him this rhetorical question, like a broken record, each question spinning into a painful crescendo.

He had besmirched his reputation enough to last for his and all of his ancestor's lifetimes. She was the nucleus, the very epicentre in his life and he had been disloyal.

Only he had the answers. He composed himself and went on his way, the scrunched up fist of guilt with a tightly woven grip around his testicles and squeezing hard throughout the remainder of his lonely journey.

Chapter 2

—⁓—

Surreptitious liaisons

Therefore, the next three months were soaked with sneaking around, surreptitious encounters and orgies of sweaty and pulsating sex. The expectation of sexual monogamy that the word marriage stands for was startlingly burnt at the stake the more they met and the more they banished their souls to the baron wastes of Cheatsville. A lonely and desperate place; where the screams of yearning, the clutches of despair are frequently heard by the divorced losers piously licking their wounds after watching their marriages dissipate before their very eyes from being caught out in affairs of this kind. It was only a matter of time before their sexual binging would bring them both careering down from the clouds of lust.

The pair were insatiable as they stole moments of earth moving nookie in their lunch hours, in the local woodland on the way back from work, down to the 'jis' drenched sheets in a grubby bed and breakfast in the back streets a few miles from their unsuspecting partners. Their trysts become more and more adventurous and daring, the stakes rising in each fling, but the burgeoning need to get their bit on the side keeping the fire burning in their affair. The seedy cogs of infidelity continued to whirr with delightful malevolence.

Raj was more than content as she had religiously pursued her 'man' and had finally got him exactly where she wanted him, sex on tap; memorable, physical and lust fuelled passion drawing her like a magnet to Manjit on a daily basis. Both of them would be lost in a haze of orgasmic duplicity from the moment they met in their trysts such was the animalistic attraction.

They became truly caught up in a turning lathe of chicanery as they both continually made up a wedge of excuses to find time to have a fleeting moment of lust with one another. Manjit would find himself pebble dashing Kully with a tirade of excuses almost like clockwork during the tenure of their affair.

Raj made a plethora of excuses ranging from going to the gym on an almost daily basis, to visiting her friends, to eating out with work colleagues, whilst Manjit expertly combined working late at the office, with playing football with the lads and evening viewings of houses as his tried and tested ruses to perform a workout of another kind.

All these spins being bought completely with not so much as a suspecting eyebrow raised. Cheating, lying, deception, trickery, back stabbing and fraudsters were all the words synonymous with this cheating pair as they stumbled from one secret tryst to another without so much as a thought about the potential for heartache their seedy liaisons would have if discovered by their partners.

Manjit would often finish off a steamy session with Raj in the bed and breakfast carefully ensuring that during the throes of passion that his lover did not dig her nails into his back or leave any other incriminating evidence on his body. This included love bites to teeth marks. This was dangerous territory and Raj played the game obediently much to Manjit's delight despite having to have her hands pinned down in one or two extremely passionate moments in their love making. On many occasions, the camera would drop downwards and a shot of them rubbing their feet together in between the sheets was all that could be seen in true Bollywood style.

Present Day – Wednesday 1st August 2007

The most memorable moment took place on a crisp August morning where like naughty school kids they had slipped away '*on meetings*' from their respective workplaces, the Estate Agency and the Beauty Salon. They had arranged to meet up in Joe's Bed and Breakfast on Bath Road in Hounslow, a regular haunt for a pulsating 20 minute bout of libidinous trouser action.

They had just finished their love making and laid there caressing each other in one another's arms. Raj stroked his left bicep and she lay her head on his chest, she circled her finger on his arm as the wave of pleasure danced around her system, flexing her toes slowly back and forward in satisfaction and wrapping her sexy brown legs around his legs. 'Babe, what's it like doing it with your missus, hmm?'

Manjit lay there, his head resting comfortably and satisfyingly on the pillow, rolled his eyes down towards her, looking at her as she stared back with her head tilted, her green eyes narrowing and with a hint of malevolence in them. 'You can't ask me that, I thought we agreed – we can't talk about our other halves...it is not right is it?'

'Yeah I know but I am just…well…curious about your relationship that's all. Why you getting so defensive about it? Just take it easy big boy.'

'Look babe what do you want me to say…hmm? That my wife is too busy like lots of wives out there, too busy to pay attention to me in the bedroom.'

'Now you are talking to me, this is what I wanted to hear.' Raj sat up on the bed and crossed her legs. It was patently clear that she was getting off on the power trip that the sensational confession was giving her, the Arcana Imperia – the secrets of the Empire revealed in perverse detail.

Manjit looked across at his mistress and could see her revelling in the finer details of his marriage, almost one notch away from frothing at the mouth such was her glee. She looked at him in wide eyed anticipation for the moment of unflinching honesty that was about to pour out of his mouth, 'well recently she is too wrapped up in stuff like going to the gym, grappling with the shopping, decorating, bringing her books home to work from her study and then there is all this socialising with her mates…and…well, leaving the odd night for us. It never used to be like this when we first got married a couple of years ago. I guess her perspective has changed now that we have settled in with one another and the honeymoon period has fizzled out into a damp squib…I guess that is the way it goes.'

Although Manjit and Kully had always been active lovers it seemed that she was now becoming overly engrossed in her work at an accountancy firm in the Treaty Centre in Hounslow and as such was not a willing participant in the physical department.

'Domesticity is the death knell of any physical kind of

relationship as all wives get too institutionalised, too cosy' he told her.

'Yeah I know she loves all that accountancy stuff. She has always been into numbers ever since we went to school together many years ago, she has not changed much then.' Raj remembered those salad days with her friend Kully when they went to Hounslow Heath Junior School and remained staunch buddies since then.

It was clear what the allure towards Raj was when speaking about his wife in the same breath. On one hand, he had a lady who was conservative, simple, non interesting and would rather flick her bean over the crunching of numbers then in a sweaty and sassy interlude with her husband. Then, sitting next to him was a stunning and utterly beguiling temptress who would relish the thought of utilising a multitude of positions in bed to satisfy her lover. A sensuous love machine who made his pulse race, took his breath away, and whose company was electrifyingly mesmerising.

He knew that he had dialled himself into this game of chance and his stylistic cheating and deception in every sense of the word resonating through every facet of his disingenuous existence.

'So when you going to leave her for me?' Raj asked excitedly. Manjit studied her face for signs of a wind up or an attempt at injecting some levity into the situation but no signs were forthcoming as she remained poker faced looking directly into his eyes.

'Ha ha, very funny, you almost had me there.' Manjit's retort was not as convincing as he would have liked, his tone punctuated with tell tale signs of trepidation and angst.

There was a silence, a deadly silence as the pair of them stared at each other uncomfortably. The current moment of unease that they both found themselves swimming in was not only upsettingly dire, but was threatening to turn ugly and rock the entire foundations of their lives. A watershed response was on the cards, the bets were very much on, and the bomb was ticking...who would draw their gun first.

Raj's eyes twitched, she narrowed them forming slits, glaring at him, her lips pursed and her brow furrowing millimetre by millimetre as time ticked on. He had held his breath for the last few moments in nervous anticipation and involuntarily let out a puff of air, still waiting and dreading the next few moments like a prisoner going to the gallows, a player in this tricky game of Russian roulette.

'Are you ever going to leave your wife for me?' her words resonating with malice and enmity. A twinge of jealousy heard in her voice and arising as if from nowhere. He biffed out some excuse about being late as he slowly slipped off the bed and started to put his trousers on, a worried expression emblazoned across his face. His actions slow and non threatening, he was trying not to unleash the hornets nest, the evil glint in her eyes being his judge and jury as the clouds of terror hung dangerously above him.

He could tangibly feel her sucking any scintilla of hope of him escaping this situation unscathed out of his quivering carcass. His feeble and desperate desire to flee the quicksand moment was being squatted like a bug. The situation had just become as predictable as the end of the Titanic film; he was going down and not in a sexually perverse way either.

She too got off the bed and walked around the bed towards him, her fingers twitching like that of a gunslinger. He was a fast dresser and had managed to slip into his shirt along with putting on his socks. His shoes teased him from across the room, enticing him to be brave and reach out for them. Raj now stood in front of him, at 5ft 2inches and with bare feet she looked up at him, the veins in her neck and forearms protruding disturbingly and her brow fully furrowed, almost sculptured with lines licking across horizontally. Her eyes narrowed with aggression.

'So you think you can just shag me anytime you want then? I thought what we had was special and maybe we had a future together? What has all this been ABOUT THEN?' Raj pushed him back hard with both her hands sending him stumbling back onto the bedside table and smashing the lamp. Her response petrifying and caked in red misted anger and rip roaring vengeance.

'Now look what you have done, you stupid...' BANG! Raj punched him straight in the face, busting his nose instantly as he fell back again onto his derriere. He clutched his nose as the blood gushed downwards. She packed a solid punch for a small girl, like a pocket rocket, her Popeye like strength was enough to deliver home the vital message that she was no-one's bit of fluff on the side. She wanted him for keeps and was not about to throw in the metaphorical towel especially now they had come this far in the proceedings.

'Why the fuck did you do that for you psycho' he spoke with anguish wiping the blood dripping from his nose with a handkerchief from his pocket and looking at her with a pained expression. You could sense the urgency in his voice, as he could not quite fathom what had just occurred. His life was dangling like a sticky and twisted jaleebi before his very eyes.

'You think you can just use me like some kind of slapper hey, click your fingers when you want to get your kicks...well I have news for you.' She leaned in close to him and dabbed her finger in a minute pool of blood that had formed on the bedside table. Raj was a strange amalgam of insecurity and possessiveness, a complex creature at the best of times.

After several dabs of the blood, she raised her finger to her mouth and flicked her tongue out licking the speck off her finger in an act of complete derangement causing Manjit to reel back in horror. 'Erm that tastes good.' She leaned back again and hissed 'you are mine now, I want you to give up your wife for me, call me when you have told her.' She then walked around the bed and started to get dressed without another word being spoken by either party.

Several moments later Raj walked out of the room and left him to clean himself up in the toilets and straighten out his nose. Her retribution had been swift and savage. The pain was still shooting up into his head. The swelling and the throbbing giving him a tight banded headache.

He put his shoes on and then sloped his needy, manipulative, cheating and duplicitous frame back towards his car in the car park. He eventually made his way back to work. The 10 minute drive gave him the much needed time to cogitate and find a way to extricate himself from this moral, ethical and hazardous dilemma. As he parked up, he dabbed at his nose again with the tissue he was holding in his hand and the last remnants of drying blood had been eradicated for good. He rummaged in his glove compartment and managed to find some soluble headache tablets. He opened the packet and thrust a couple of bad boys straight down the hatch.

He rested his head back on the head rest of the car and looked wistfully out of the window. Which way could he turn now? It had been 3 months of sneaking around with relentless toe curling sex, whilst all the time deceiving his wife, pissing on the very nucleus and tenets of their marriage – trust, integrity, loyalty and openness. His disease of stupidity in embarking upon this treacherous road was haunting him at every given turn; it seemed now, after witnessing the psychotic behaviour displayed to him by Raj that there was little or no escape from this sinking quagmire.

He thumped the steering wheel with his right fist. All of a sudden, his mobile phone rang out. He reached into his pocket and looked at the display. It was Raj. His gait scowled disgust as he threw the phone down on the seat next to him. What did she want with him now? The punch had been the death knell in their relationship; it was the moment when he had decided enough was enough, the time when she had turned from sexy mistress into the apostle of Satan. It was over. The next 10 minutes flew by as he remained sat in his car. He looked at the caller display on the phone; there were 7 missed calls from the possessed and crazy Raj. She was on high stalking alert and it seemed that she wanted to finish the job off literally, but the calls continued to be screened.

A few more moments passed and he got out of the car scooping up the mobile with him and walked into the office like a boxer returning to his corner after having gone a few rounds with Mike Tyson such was the state of his hooter. He suppressed his urge to shout 'yo Adrian' as he walked up to his desk, seeing the slightly humorous side of being belted by a 5ft 2inch nutter he thought. He nestled into his seat and looked across the desk at the photo of him and Kully hugging tightly on a holiday snap taken last year in Egypt – the majestic Pyramids towering behind them as Kully's arms romantically draped around her hubby. He smiled and then reached out and stroked his wife's face on the photo. His affair had hit the buffers, he had now had his fun, his 2 year itch, or whatever it was, now was the time to be 'sidaa saada (straight).

He turned in his chair and looked over at Bill his gora (English) work colleague as he sat there chatting to a client on the phone and patently oblivious to his presence and then glanced out of the window. His eyes widened in utter disbelief as a car trawled slowly past the shop front, 5mph, inching past. The driver was none other than Raj, how could he mistake her, after all he now knew every inch of her, warts and all.

She waved menacingly at him as she snaked past. Her eyes still forming narrow slits, as was the case in the bedroom, and her face, one that Medusa would have been proud. Her sinister appearance jolted Manjit to his very core. He sat up in the chair as she floated past in her car / broomstick on her way to her workplace. They say you can dance with the devil but it is very much at your own risk.

She was sending a message to him and that message was going to become all too apparent in the next few minutes when his life would be turned on it's head and the metaphorical rug yanked cleanly from under his duplicitous feet…

CHAPTER 3

Risky business

The clasp and charm of the affair had died, it seemed that they had both got what they set out to achieve, the thrill and excitement, the initial novelty of the chase was now far too risqué for them. Manjit had dipped his toe into the lake of infidelity and had lived to tell the tale and with sexually satisfying memories imprinted within his frames of reference as a keepsake.

The writing was on the wall, he had crossed over into murky waters and he was sinking fast. The boisterous behaviour now replaced by trepidation and loneliness as he contemplated his imminent demise from his sordid relations with his mistress. He was only now beginning to realise that he had tangoed with the wrong devil, his idealism of a small illicit liaison was now his very undoing, the furtive affair set on a timer and ready to explode in his face and merely a snitching phone call away.

Nestled into his seat behind his desk, the predictable malaise of the office making his skin hot and clammy, but a feeling of intense satisfaction emblazoned emphatically across his face, despite the continual throbbing sensation from his nose. He walked over to the toilet at the rear of the agency and surveyed the damage in the mirror. It did not look too bad and he would certainly be able to 'get away' with it when at home later that evening, that was the most crucial aspect of this escapade. A trickle of edification swept across his body along with the catharsis that came along with the knowledge that he had shared his last bed with his demented lover.

He looked back at the picture of Kully in a snap taken last month that had marked their 2nd wedding anniversary. His stomach twisted for a second, her beautiful smile radiating out of the photo and slapping his face with shameful sin. He knew that he had already let her down, let himself down and especially in the year that they had planned to try for a baby, what had he been thinking of when he first embarked upon this sleazy affair with his mistress?

Kully was everything he could have wished for in a wife and more, she was good looking, possessed a warm personality, a caring nature and above all she adored him.

Manjit remained pensive staring at the photo some more; he reached out and stroked her face with his guilt ridden fingers. He knew that the fun was over, he had to move on; he simply could not hurt her anymore. He looked around the office, the other co-workers were busily working away with their daily tasks, answering the telephone and wrestling with their computer keyboards. He looked back and his boss was absent, out on business, the coast was clear. He took his mobile out of his pocket, toggled to Raj, and initiated the call.

'Hello sexy you missing me already?' she whispered, being cautious not to unduly alert her assistants in the Beauty salon *'Princesses Parlour'* that she owned and worked in the Treaty Centre (the very nucleus of

Hounslow). It sounded more like a house of ill repute then a place where you could get your nails and hair done for a few shillings.

In a moment of fine cinematic masterpiece he rose like a Punjabi dhol player from the ashes 'listen Raj – I think we should just cool things, don't you think? It is getting far too risky.'

His opening gambit was met with an uneasy silence. He knew that she would not respond favourably to him calling off their secret liaison, but the deadly silence somehow lent a more sinister and unsettling malevolence to the moment. 'You still there?' Manjit enquired, a sense of trepidation lingering in his tone. He knew that the next few minutes would require all the skill and vigour that he could muster to attempt to beguile his mistress.

'What do you mean cool it for a bit?' You mean a few weeks or something?' She responded, finally in a somewhat obtuse manner.

Manjit moved the phone to the other ear and placed his hand over the mouth piece flitting his eyes up to see if any of the other creatures in the office were eaves dropping in a bid to bring some much needed excitement into their lives with some hot gossip. To date their affair had been kept hush hush from all prying eyes.

Manjit had diced with danger for far too long and precariously; he was in the very salubrious and enviable situation whereby he was serving up a couple of pieces of fresh Indian meat on alternate days with all the intense satisfaction that comes along with such liaisons.

Manjit whispered down the phone 'lets cool it, what we had was memorable and great but it has to stop now, all I want more than anything is my own kid and to make my wife happy. Our relationship is done, face up to that and realistically we have both got what we wanted for the short time it lasted, let's be adult about this and move on with our own respective relationships.'

His advice was sound, and any normal person would understand that the thrill was had, it was all done and cooked and it was sensibly time to move on. His testosterone burning days with his lover were concluded.

Raj however was the very anthesis of sensibility as her damning response proved 'I won't let you go, it is not anyone I have casual sex with you know. You think you can just call the shots and dump me when you are satisfied? How about all those things you said to me in bed, all those intimate moments we had, surely they had to mean something. I am not some kuti slag you can drop when you want. I could get a string of fellas after me. I won't let you go.' She failed to come up for air as her verbal onslaught continued.

She was not responding to the news as well as he thought she would. She was a vexation to his already flagging spirit and he had to remove this additional and unwelcomed baggage from his life finally.

He had made his point quite clear, his slate was clean and he was keen to slither back into his humdrum and normal lifestyle after having got his sexual kicks, totally undetected.

'I am warning you! You had better tell your wife about us or you will be sorry. All those times in bed when you told me you loved me had to mean something. Babe you are just in denial.' Her voice became more menacing and threatening as she continued 'anyway you know my husband will go crazy when I tell him about how you just took advantage of me.' Her threat reverberated around the room.

'You are so ruthless aren't you? It is surreal.' Manjit replied.

'You have to be in this life, simple as that.' Raj was decisive with her come back.

A decision had to be made and he replied patiently ''listen don't talk crazy, it is best if we just let sleeping dogs lie if you catch my drift, we have had our bit of fun and let's forget it ever happened, okay?' There was a discernible tremor in his voice when he spoke. Manjit was patently trying to buck the trend of continuing to cheat and deceive his wife with his fancy woman as many before him have done so in similar circumstances.

Raj shook her head and growled back 'right you arsehole,' her retort sublimely gauche and taking him by surprise.

'Look it is over!' Manjit cut over her swiftly 'this is it – just stay out of my life from now on okay…I will not answer your calls and if you do say anything to my wife or your husband then I will deny it anyway, okay…so stay away please.'

He depressed the button on his mobile and slowly let the phone hang down into the palm of his hand, pressing the tip of it into his forehead and leaning forward resting his elbow onto the desk. He sat there stiff with fear for a moment and thought about the exchange they had just had. It was the right thing to do; he was confused as to why he had ever let himself down by embarking on such a risky and deplorable minefield as that of having an affair, why?

Only he knew the answers with the obvious one being – that he was a guy and that was, well, what guys do isn't it?

He placed the phone on the table and stared down at his own sweaty hand as it had a mind of its own, shaking all along. His body jittery and jolting with adrenaline. He had always possessed a nervous shake when the heat got too much in the kitchen; it was his inability to control the adrenaline surging through his veins on his body. His hand continued to shake uncontrollably as he steadied it on the desk in front of him.

He had been bold and audacious but he was sure that it was the best decision he had ever made, after all, he truly loved Kully with all his heart.

Manjit wiped the sweat from his brow with his sleeve and dialled the number for home, hoping to catch his doting wife Kully. She had taken the day off to catch up on things at home and to earn a timely release from the spinning wheel she had found herself in all too recently with her accountancy workload.

She had earlier booked herself in for a massage, a manicure and pedicure from Raj's salon, as an ex gratia treat from her oldest school friend. Thankfully, Kully had already been and gone an hour or so before Raj had returned after having been on her back with her legs in the air in the Bed and Breakfast and with Kully's very own husband to exacerbate matters. (Now that was worth the concession Raj thought as she ran her claws through Manjit's shock of hair in their tryst).

Kully answered after a few rings and Manjit composed himself trying not to let any signs of his duplicity seep through into his voice and ring alarm bells from his missus. 'You okay gorgeous, what you up to?' he asked.

There are two ways a guy can go when he is getting it from an outside source, he will either be extremely nice to you, from flowers, to compliments, and who can blame him he is getting to sleep with two woman at the same time and who knows maybe more – depending on his organisational skills and juggling capabilities.

Manjit was displaying this smokescreen in emphatic fashion and anyone would have struggled to decipher that he only just had his orgasmic kicks from another honey pot. His wife was not suspicious throughout which was a welcome starter for ten for him. Manjit was not a cheater per se. It seemed he had just been the victim of the classic opportunist snare. The one that buckles the legs of the staunchest of married guys from time to time. His ideological tilt had been well ingrained over years of seeing, hearing the experiences of others who had slithered down the same black hole, and now here he was, another victim washed up on the sandy shores of duplicity.

Kully smiled, she always liked it when her hubby called her during an otherwise routine day at the office. It was different and solidified her love for him, even more especially when it was just a social call. 'Hi ya, how's work?' she enquired.

'Yeah I have been in the office all morning stuck behind the computer screen, the phone has been ringing non stop.' His prevarication providing the quintessential swindle and deception in this moment. He had thought a few steps ahead and had countered any future finger pointing accusations, any heart stopping incriminations about him getting his leg over in the morning with his twisted lover. After all, how could he have done so when his wife '*knew*' that in actual fact her unswerving husband was busy working away like a trooper since the break of day, earning a hard earned crust for them. The subterfuge worked like a dream. 'Ahhh don't worry hun

I will make us a nice dinner tonight, okay.' her dulcet tones soothing him like a warm blanket.

Manjit responded whilst simultaneously fighting off the slush of guilt that was once again creeping into his voice 'I just want to say I love you babe...I...well...I don't tell you often enough but I am so glad I am with you and no-one else, you really pump my tyres.'

The line was crass and most punters would be reaching out for the bucket, but Kully digged the comment chiming back 'don't worry you will have plenty of time to show me how much you love me tonight, after they have gone.'

He yearned to return to his own feathered nest with his girl and leave the mucus trail of sneaky sex behind him finally.

Manjit listened intently with a confused hue on his face 'After who have gone?' Maybe he had missed something as he sought clarity with his question.

Kully flipped the phone to the other ear and held it in place with her shoulder momentarily as she filled the kettle with water in her kitchen, hoping to put her feet up with a soothing cup of 'chaa' on her day off. She replied 'oh yeah I have invited your brother and his missus over for dinner tonight, rather than just cook for us it will be nice, don't you think?'

'What, you have done what?' Manjit's response was terrifying and melodramatic. 'I was, err, hoping we could just relax in front of the box or something.'

His sang froid was shattered in one foul swoop. He continued with his unequivocal outburst 'oh that is great, I just don't need that after the day I have had.

You don't understand love I just want to relax and am not in the mood to entertain.' He dabbed his nose again with the handkerchief he had taken hold of from his jacket pocket, and in that second, getting a flashback from the earlier smack he had received from '*Raj Marciano.*'

It was clear that Manjit's anguish was brought on solely from his earlier one sided boxing match and overall relief of kissing goodbye to his sordid three monthly affair. He was like any other man, he just wanted a quiet beer, some good homely company and a chance to turn a fresh chapter in his life. Was that too much to ask?

It apparently was as Kully remained staunch 'come on it won't be that bad, we haven't seen them in a while and I think it will be nice to have a few beers especially before the next couple of nights.'

Once again, Manjit appeared quizzical whilst slipping an extra chewing gum in his mouth from an open packet lying on his desk. He crunched on the gum for a couple of seconds as the cogs whirled in his head before asking 'what is happening in the next few days? I have a brain like a goldfish.'

Kully laughed 'I know you have! Well tonight we have dinner as you know and on Friday it is guess who's birthday?'

Manjit thought for a second 'oh, what a doofus, of course it is my older bruvs birthday.'

Kully 'yep and we have a dinner party around his house and then on Saturday we have all planned the girls night in over at Tej's house with you rascals going out in town.'

Manjit's oaf like brain quickly caught up and registered with the itinerary as it came flooding back to him from his ball and chains timely reminders.

'Boys night out on Saturday, that will be a good one. He added with the ebullience of a child.

'Okay don't be late tonight. We are expecting them at 7pm.'

Kully terminated the phone call as did an apathetic Manjit before he lounged back in his office chair cogitating hard about the dinner date in the evening. He was not in the mood and it promised to be a total disaster movie. The long leash of marriage was being yanked and this kuta was obediently dancing to the tune of his master.

The working day ticked by and the thoughts oscillated in his mind all the time. He looked at his watch, only 2 hours to go. The nearer the dinner date loomed, his thoughts and feeling of being sucked deeper and deeper into something he just did not want to face burgeoning. Although he loved his brother, he had just had the juice schlurped out of him this morning and his bruv was a wild, unpredictable and lively character at the best of times, far too crazy for the unnervingly petrified Manjit...

Chapter 4

—⁓—

Sleeping dogs lie

Manjit clipped his hands free hub to his ear and connected the blue tooth to his mobile phone as he sat in his car. He summoned up 'Saty' his loyal friend. He started the engine of his sexy and sleek BMW and reversed out of the car park bay, heading out to the main road. The phone rang several times before it was answered 'kidda Saty you busy, can you talk?' Manjit enquired.

He had got to know Saty through his wife's friendship with Saty's missus Tejinder. The girls had remained staunch friends since attending the same schools in Hounslow, and as was inevitable the husbands hit it off in the many drink and dinner dates that ensued after that.

Saty had been unemployed for a few years after having been made redundant from a local computer company after they went bust. His inherent and slovenly attitude to getting back into work and being gainfully employed again was always a topic of concern and discussion in his relationship. He much preferred being a man of leisure and the thought of galvanising himself back to work was enough to get his 34 year old frame jittery and make his eyes bleed.

Amongst his most endearing features were his short wavy black perm hairstyle draped over his skull like a weathered and heavily bleached mop. This was coupled with a sinewy body and round ball shaped face. His snorting pig like laugh and garden gnome 5ft 2inch size was just about intimidating as some of the worker ants in his garden. His other famed features including his hairy tarantula ears and gorilla covered body with hair sprouting out in places where it was just humanly impossible to grow hair, such as the follicle that protruded from his eyeball a few years ago.

It took a mammoth team effort of tugging and yanking from Manjit and others to extract the imposter despite the blood curdling screams from the downtrodden and hirsute monkey boy who they held down on the ground with there sneakers firmly pressed on his throat for added security. It worked with his eyeball only just about remaining in its socket by the tiniest of fibres. But hey that is what mates are for.

Saty and Tejinder had been blissfully married for 4 salubrious years without even the slightest sniff of an argument spoiling the ambience. They were like a couple of old slippers. They were so in love that you could just imagine them licking the little traces of sleep out of one another's eyes during the throes of passion, or cutting each other's toe nails without a bat of the eye lid. Unemployment had unfortunately brought out the worst in Saty as his vegetative habits had exacerbated from his slouching around the house all day, biting his nails, picking his nose, belching and farting amongst the prime contenders on the ever burgeoning list, not to mention his tufts of hair being left around the house when his body hair was moulting.

Manjit and Saty had a good understanding with one another and in some respects Manjit relied on his friend as a reliable confidant, the kind of 'dosta with the mosta.'

Saty replied 'yeah what's up mate?'

'Nothing I just wanted to chew your ear about something.' Manjit got straight to the point.

'Cool, what's up?' came the reply from his friend. He sounded unfailingly chirpy.

'My life is turning into a Greek tragedy. You know I have been checking out this girl for a bit, the one who is married, well she is turning into a bit of a bunny boiler, all possessive and clingy and I think she is looking to stir the pot especially now that I want to cool the flames a bit, what should I do mate?' Saty knew of the affair but not precisely who the individual concerned was as this would have been far too risky.

Saty made a sucking sound with his lips as he took a long intake of breath. 'Mate I am not being funny with you but seriously there is fishing bait out there that could decipher the difference between looking and touching, I mean come on mate hey. What did you expect to happen?' Saty was direct with his criticism for his friend. 'Yeah I know that now,' he responded apathetically.

Saty advised his friend some more and chipped back 'well...don't do nothing stupid and break it off right away, cos if you do, well I don't think it will do much for her ego and she might cause you a bit of grief, what is stopping her phoning your missus right now and confessing?'

His words piercing through Manjit's heart with ground shattering reality. Manjit, recognizing the warning sign asked 'but surely she has got too much to lose if she did spill the beans on me, right?' His rhetorical question hung feebly in the air as he continued 'nah she wouldn't do that, I know her… at least I think, nah she will just throw a hissy fit and move on with her life.'

Manjit was not only trying sheepishly to convince Saty but also himself. He was desperately seeking the flimsiest crumb of comfort to be tossed his way, but the loud knocking sound reverberating throughout Manjit's head was the haunting sounds of the divorce court the longer he mused the ramifications of his recent phone call with his mistress.

Saty sensing his friends despair, did what any true friend would do and seized the opportunity to wind his buddy up a bit more, turn the screw another notch and sink his fangs in one final swish. 'Yeah she will probably phone your missus and then tell her hubby, totally blaming it all on you saying that you tried to seduce her and all that just to see what substance he is made out of. Also whether he has the minerals to come over to yours and dish out the beating of your life, I mean proper licks, ha ha.' Saty cackled heartily with his sinister Amrish Puri like laugh seemingly going on for days. Manjit was meanwhile shaking his head in disappointment on the other end of the line. He was incredulous that his pleas were being mocked and ridiculed with irrelevant levity.

He piped up quickly nipping Saty's marauding comedy army in the bud, well thanks for that, I feel a lot better already…seriously if you are going to muck about then I won't bother, what do I do? I mean seriously, she DID NOT TAKE THE NEWS WELL.' Manjit found himself raising his voice to emphasise the reason for the SOS phone call in the first instance.

'Seriously, is she calm now though?' Saty enquired before preparing himself to offer his soothing words of advice that were much needed in this situation.

'Calm, you are joking right? She is about as calm as the Incredible Hulk after he has popped a bottle of steroids, sunk ten cans of Red Bull and snorted a couple of lines of coke, basically not very tranquil.' Manjit's response leaving his friend in no doubt as to the ladies temperament and state of mind at the present time.

This seemed to assuage any further teasing and sporadic bouts of humour from Coco the Clown. He responded immediately, cool headed and with a more soothing voice, after all they had known each other long enough to detect when the other was teetering on the edge of desperation. 'Okay, this is what you do...leave it a day and call her in the morning, she will have calmed down considerably.'

Manjit listened intently, this was the rub, the reason why he had called.

Saty continued 'if she is calm, explain that you have got too much to lose and that it is a hundred per cent over and that you will have to take the secret to your graves or too many others will get hurt in the process, that I am certain will appeal to her sensitive side.'

Manjit egged him on 'yeah yeah go on.'

'then just when she is lapping it up tell her that she gave him the best sex ever and you will never forget it, bang, then she will leave with that satisfying memory...you have then got sure fire reassurance that she will walk away with her pride intact and less likely to turn your life upside down.'

Manjit listened on eagerly 'but how does that work in theory, what is stopping her from spurting out the truth to our other halves?'

Saty, who during this exchange was passing himself off well as some kind of seasoned, Chinese Grandmaster. The kind who sits on a rock in a jungle somewhere, and flicks his long wavy hair under a cascading waterfall just like a Timotei advert and who would pass On his God given wisdom to the hoi polloi down below.

He soothingly replied' this is because you always have to give her an outer, a way out of the situation, a glimmer of spin so that she is the one who is calling the shots – NOT YOU…if she thinks she is a cornered rat then she will go for your jugular, without question my friend.'

'Okay, okay.' Manjit lapped up the advice with the speed of a malnutritioned cat being offered a saucer of milk.

'The only thing I will say is have you taken care of the audit trail?'

'What audit trail?' he asked.

'I am talking about anything that will lead back to you having an affair you fool, emails, text messages, last dialled numbers, knickers in your pocket, friends who have seen you together, blah blah, you get me?' his friend's benevolence had not gone amiss as Manjit responded.

'Yeah I think so. I normally phone her from work so that is covered. I haven't got any knickers either. That was basically because she didn't wear any when she saw me.' Saty chipped in 'get out of here, you jammy bastard. Is she an Indian girl?'

'Yeah, I know, I just asked her once not to bother and that was it she never wore them again, it was well cool.'

'You sure you want to end this?'

'I know, I know, I have to, she is getting a bit too clingy and comfortable now, I mean too many questions. We have got to that stage when the honeymoon period of the affair is gone, you know the chase is gone, the hunter has just brought a pair of slippers and is happy lounging around the fire with his mistress...'

'You crazy if I had a girl - an Indian girl, who come on a date with me without knickers on, and of course I was not married then I would be up there like a squirrel up a tree, proper fast.'

'Yeah true, but I reckon worse case scenario even if for any reason she ever did tell my wife, you know just imagine this is as bad as it has got and my missus is standing there with the rolling pin in her hand then I will do what every Asian guy would do in that situation, standard.'

'What's that?'

'Denial - it was not me. What you talking about? She has been after me for ages, she is stalking me and all the other bull crap that I can muster up at that precise moment. I will just deny it to such an extent that I will actually start believing it myself, so that I will have to dig real deep into my frame of reference to savour those knickerless moments of sex that I enjoyed with her. That is the ace up my sleeve and it is obvious that if I create that element of doubt in my wife's brain...then who do you think she is likely to believe?'

'Good point, she won't have any proof if you never sent any text messages and all that, but all I will say is stop messing around with your girl, she is a diamond and a kuta like you shouldn't arse about with her, that is just my opinion for what it is worth.' Saty's advice sent a stern message through to his friend, a friendly kick up the derriere that was long over due.

'Thanks man, I appreciate the advice, look I am almost home now, I will chat to you later, but thanks again.' Manjit showed his appreciation.

'Anytime, let me know how it is going okay.'

'Damn straight, will do, take it easy, thanks.' With that, Manjit cut the call and pulled up outside his house. He felt his skin clammy, hot and sticky as he sucked in some air through his mouth.

A fiery combination of nervous anticipation in seeing his wife, and the catharsis that had followed the conclusion of his murky affair, resonating throughout his body.

He slithered up the drive slowly, beeping the car alarm behind him, the lights of his car flashing and then dimming. He wiped his brow in a bid to conceal the cheap stench of sex from his affair from incriminating himself any further. His wife was a smart cookie and the wrong look, an awkward glance to a question; in fact, any shed of evidence would be obvious and excruciatingly painful from the standard swipe in the testicles that would follow suit should he be found with the smoking gun in his paw.

—☙—

CHAPTER 5

Flirting with flames

Rita had developed close feelings for Amar over the 6 months or so that they had been working together at Desi's Solicitors. This was not through choice but almost a freakish coincidence as this was the exact time span that her marriage has been strained and at near breaking point several times over, and of course like any ruthless coyote, Amar was a more than willing recipient to let her cry on his manly shoulders.

The solicitors practice was initially set up by two brothers Davinder and Pradeep Bansal and established in the community for over 20 years, they were consummate experts in all fields of the legal trade and had eked out an impressive existence in their manor.

Rita had been at the firm for 2 years since she had got married to Gaurav and left her family home back in Bristol. She worked alongside the dark and handsome Amar who had been earning his salary as a trainee solicitor.

Amar, standing at 6ft 1inch, a short crew cut, clean shaven with a neck like a pit-bull. His muscular physique, his 28 years of street savvy, the entire package making him a modern day Adonis with his smoking hot muscles.

His devoutness and talent in the study of the ancient martial arts of Kung Fu naturally complimenting his strength and conviction. This freak of nature was as big and fearsome as a butcher's dog. He was no stranger to violence and with a black Sash marking his skill in his chosen art stirring his confidence and fighting ability ten fold he was not afraid of anyone or anything. He was a sneering malevolent kind of guy if the opportunity ever presented itself, and more often than not, his ability was rigorously tested in a flood of situations.

Growing up on the murky streets of Slough had been the sandbox where he had cut his teeth in the days of green. This pugnacious and uncompromising fella had enough cuts and scars on his physique to back up his claims of a tough and unrelenting upbringing.

Amar was the sort of animal who got exactly what he wanted out of life. There were no ifs or buts just, a solid and sedulous pursuit of his goals no matter what they were, cars, money, sporting achievements and even your wife, yes that's right, there was not a scintilla of remorse when focussing his endeavours on another's partner, and this was the fuel that motivated this hungry hound.

Then one time, a few months ago, they had met up after work in Bar Bhangra their local pub to wind down after a stressful day where they had been grafting like trojan's from sunrise to sunset.

Their conversation ebbed and flowed as it always did, both of them revelling in one another's company. They had a connection of sorts in an atmosphere of candour did these flamboyant socialites.

Rita chatted away with Amar sitting across from her on the table. She was a Hindu Punjabi girl, 31 years old, standing at 5 ft 6 inches tall; an impressive stature for an Indian girl with her penchant for high heels making her tower at a monstrous 5ft 8inches on most days. This was considered tall for an Asian girl especially as the average height for an Asian girl remained at a modest 5ft 4 inches.

There was an indefinable '*cor*' about her, a certain allure. Her strongly fragranced perfume pleasantly raising the goosebumps on his tree trunk type arms. Her legs, smooth, silky and fair adding the salsa sauce to her lascivious appearance. She was a head turner.

A Pimms and lemonade and Cobra beer kept them both company. The usual conversational pleasantries exchanged, the plethora of anecdotal memories about the other staff at the practice making them chortle uncontrollably, despite Amar only having graced the solicitors practice for a short period of time and still a relative greenhorn.

'So come on then spill the beans then treacle.' Amar took a swig from his beer, his eyes looking at Rita over the rim of the pint glass and studying her reaction to the question. Rita looked at him with a confusion etched face 'what beans?' she enquired, her quizzical look continuing.

'Playing hardball, I like your style.' Okay...' he leaned forward on the table gently picking up his pint glass and placing it to the side so that he could rest his hands, clasped together in front of him on the table surface. He explained himself 'you made a comment last week about your husband still being a twat. Is he messing you about even more?' Rita's eyes widened and she shook her head in a defeatist manner.

Amar sensing this quickly elaborated 'I overheard you talking to...err what's her name...Kully on the phone...well...you were going to town on him I must say. As a betting man I would say that he is still up to his old tricks of having affairs, the low life piece of scum.' Amar had never hid the fact that he completely and utterly despised her husband as his fulminating onslaught depicted. Rita raised the glass to her mouth, paused for a nano second before necking the entire contents, slowly placing the glass back on the table.

Amar was everything her husband wasn't, loyal, seemingly trustworthy, rough and ready, brutishly strong, understanding, passionate and with a certain ruthlessness surrounding his every action. Rita had always had a disposition for the rufty tufty guys, and had dated her fair share as she was growing up. In fact the wilder the better was her motto back then.

The normal, stay at home, Guinness slipper wearing, Ovaltine drinking nerds need not apply, nor those who had a particular penchant and hankering to sleep around. This cat had always wanted hot and pulsating action between the sheets, but from someone she truly connected with, this was a pre requisite. What she despised more than anything were duplicitous cheaters, congenial liars and guys shagging around with other fillies, when they were meant to be with her. It was a pride thing and a tenet that she had clung on to dearly since knee high to a grasshopper.

Rita inspected Amar's face, it smacked of a mask of rapture and devilish virility. It also told the story of a hard upbringing, a tough and unrelenting life, but more sinisterly, a world of mayhem that accompanied this battle hardened soldiers every step. This was as vivid as the track being played out of the Punjabi jukebox behind them *'Mundiya tah bachke rahaye'(beware of the boys) as* they sat in momentary silence, their passionate and fiery attachment simply electrifying. Then she averted her eyes across the room and slunk back in her chair diffusing the chemistry that was gripping them.

Amar reciprocated whilst swiftly ditching the thoughts of chandelier swinging nookie with his fantasy woman for the moment.

She was drawn to him like a moth to a flame and had been ever since he first stumbled into the work place months ago. The drink in her system amplified these feelings as she crossed and uncrossed her legs pointing her knee towards him, whilst flicking her hair back over her shoulder – two sure fire non verbal signals that a woman wants your kittens if there were any. Amar, the wily fox, knew this too as he got up and moved his chair around the table and sat next to Rita, she did not seem too disturbed by this manoeuvre and her expression was a welcoming and open invitation for him to do just that.

He continued 'not everything is cool between you too, is it?' his question smooth but purposefully searching.

He was hoping that the combination of drink streaming through her body, the availability of his broad shoulders for support and his succinct probing would be the perfect fusion for the ceremonial opening of the truth floodgates in this sublimely calculated moment of ensnarement.

Rita's surprise continued 'yeah I don't really want to talk about it, it is my business, my bed and I have to lie on it, you know what I mean.' The pain and torment could clearly be heard in Rita's voice. She was on the precipice of an earth shattering split from her spouse as her 2 year *'marriage'* was very much on the rocks. She knew herself too well and that one Freudian slip, one insight into her anguish, and her verbosity would signal the affirmation and death knell on her relationship.

Rita knew that the die had been cast when Gaurav her husband had cheated on her several times throughout the short tenure of their marriage. They say that first impressions can be deceptive as was the case when they had courted for a short time before he had popped the question in Kew Gardens of all places. She was marrying a good looking and overtly caring husband, or so she thought.

She quickly learnt that he had a reputation with the girls and with his boyish good looks, slender 6ft body with accompanying six pack honed to perfection over his 31 years he never had too much trouble in enticing man eating students in the gym he worked at as a personal fitness instructor. The young impressionable felines would throw their quaking bodies at him for a workout of another kind after hours, and with no wedding ring on his finger to deter them the bait was always set with confidence.

The trouble was that he was like most guys who were offered – N.S.A (no stings attached) sex, they dived in hammer and tongs and indulged without a care for the consequences. The bigger and juicier the carrot the more guys like Gaurav had to fulfil their personal sex odyssey.

The longer they remained together, the longer he had failed to curb his roving eye for the ladies with his irrational and bitter condemnation for staying monogamous for the sake of future marital bliss, despite having 'a looker' like Rita on his arm as his wife. It seemed that some guys were insatiable when the secondary brain was engaged, preferring instead to get their kicks from thrilling and forbidden passion elsewhere.

Amar, like any would be predator had been lurking surreptitiously in the shadows of their fragile relationship continued to listen intently to all her woes, day in day out, especially when the tormented wife exuded the kind of class and beauty that Rita did.

It was a wise move for him as he fantasised about her every night, from the moment the first crack had appeared in his prey's relationship. It was just a matter of time before he would pounce and scoop up his winnings.

'Look you can talk to me; I am not your husband.' Amar reached over and held Rita's hands, gripping them tightly, his motions naturally driven by romantic and lust fuelled urges. His mercenary intent not distinguishable to Rita.

'You know I have got marriage problems, I just don't know what to do anymore. He will never change, I know that and he knows that.' she replied in downcast and gloomy resignation. Another hapless victim on the horror express on the rough terrain of an affair. Her eyes narrowing and exquisitely warding off the barrage of thick and frothy tears that were threatening to explode out of her sockets.

Amar sensed this and rapidly placed his arm over her shoulder and around her back pulling her into him. His draping arm, squeezing her tight to his chest. She did not resist and placed her head on his chest. She could hear his heart beating fast and thumping against her face through his shirt. His ability to sustain and comfort her in turbulent times scoring him the necessary brownie points on the predatory checklist as he sent in the reinforcement of his other arm. He now had both arms wrapped around her tightly pulling her in to him, with one of his hands rubbing her back gently.

After a few moments they separated, a new found bond emerging from an otherwise tumultuous outpouring from Rita. She got up and scuttled to the toilet, the tears stinging her eyes as they finally erupted like an angry volcano. Why was she shedding tears for him? He was a lothario, a Don Juan who would never change. She crashed into the toilet, her mascara running down her cheeks. She sat on the toilet seat shutting the cubicle door behind her, her need to reflect in the dark, solitary and silent world that a public cubicle lends was comforting.

After 10 minutes or so she emerged, she looked across the pub floor; Amar was still there waiting patiently and with a look of concern. They exchanged a few words before leaving Bar Bhangra. They walked into the car park situated opposite. Their eyes met a last time, a lingering look under the cloudless blue skies as they set off in their respective cars going separate ways.

Amar's pad was a des res in a leafier part of nearby Slough. A home he shared with his parents. Meanwhile Rita had the savouring prospect of returning to her 2 bedroom flat she shared with Gaurav on Staines Road complete with piss soaked stairwells and bucketfuls of heroin needles strewn on the steps leading to her castle.

They had been saving up enough money, earlier on in their marriage for a deposit on a house. They were still some time away from fulfilling their dream of buying a salubrious des res, although, this particular ideology was firmly put on hold due to the strains and cracks seeping into their relationship. Rita looked back at him once more. There was an animal attraction between them as they both tried desperately to stifle their burgeoning feelings for one another despite her loins itching and burning like a forest fire...

CHAPTER 6

—₥—

'Whores' d'oeuvres

The doorbell rang at the residence of Manjit and Kully. It was 7pm on the nose and the invited couple were impeccably on time, going against the time held Indian tradition of being an hour or so later than the advertised time.

Manjit was sat on the sofa watching some television having earlier weathered the concerned looks from Kully when she had enquired about his nose looking like a piece of red swollen meat. He had fenced clever by making up a story about a work colleague accidentally slamming a door on his face earlier and that it was no big deal. After all lying and cheating his way out of situations had become his specialist *'Mastermind'* subject of late. Kully ambled from the kitchen and opened the door to her guests.

Standing in the crisp and balmy plume of the evening air were Manjit's brother Hardeep and his loving wife, an old school friend of Kully's and along with Tejinder, they had all graced the same local junior school, growing up as a tightly woven clique. She welcomed them in, a kiss on the cheek for the pair as they stumbled over the threshold. Manjit meanwhile stood up in the living room having heard the excited banter from the hallway as he waited to welcome and embrace his guests for the evening. His hand began to shake uncontrollably as he sought to tame the beast by placing it in his pocket. A usual occurrence when in situations of torment or anxiety. He was conscious not to unduly disconcert his guests as they walked in with visions of his hand vigorously shaking in his pocket and with a toothy smile on his face at the same time – in some countries you could be arrested for that.

Moments later the door to the living room opened and in entered Hardeep, his elder brother, a 32 years old mobile phone worker. The musky smell of cologne filling the room as he stepped forward. His hairline rapidly receding at the front, his face punctuated with small features, his narrow eyes (The demonic and implacable eyes of a mad man Manjit would tease him as they grew up) His chubby cheeks and blob of a nose all hiding the belligerent and unrelenting fury swimming as an under current of his outwardly friendly nature. His wife had been the calming influence in his life since their marriage some 3 years ago with his hot temper curbed with the shackles of responsibility weighing him down like an anchor.

'Kidda sunshine.' Hardeep hugged his little brother, embracing him with his portly 5ft 10 inch frame and like a python temporarily squeezing the air out of Manjit's already weakened body and lungs. They had last seen each other a few weeks ago and now with events and dates poised; as they were, it would be three meetings in succession. This was no problem as the brothers got on like the proverbial house on fire. Their scraps memorable throughout the years, attacks with scissors, good old fashioned fist fights and even threats to kill each other all blighting an otherwise tightly bound relationship, it was just what brothers did – fight. The respect between them was no doubt undeniable.

Manjit handed his brother a tumbler with Jack Daniels and coke, it was what they both drank and they clinked their glasses with Hardeep throwing his body onto the sofa leaving Manjit standing in the centre of the room and strangely anxious, his skittish mannerisms unsettling. He heard the girls talking in the hallway, the voices becoming louder and nearer as Kully walked through first smiling. Trailing behind Hardeep's wife, the irrepressible Rajinderpal – or Raj to me, you and Manjit. Yes, the same one that Manjit had been treating like a whore in Joe's Bed and Breakfast earlier that morning.

In she walked like a death sentence, like the princess of darkness. Manjit remained earnest and uptight. His trepidation exacerbating ten fold at the mere sight of the temptress.

As she emerged, he cast his eyes over her black figure hugging dress accentuating her breasts, her legs as smooth as they had been when he was running his tongue up and down them with unbridled satisfaction. The black criss cross heeled shoes gently elevating her feet and showing off her toned and curvaceous calves. She looked stunning and with her face flush with pride and knife twisting satisfaction.

If you thought it impossible to see a man visibly go weak at the knees, dribble incessantly and hold up a white flag in resignation then this was the situation developing right here and right now.

His emotions continually churning, a fusion of impending doom and the classic 'what happened next scenario?'

There was a reason for his apathy in the office, when the dinner date had been arranged by his wife. It was his fear of his dark and deep rooted secret being laid bare before his would be executioners.

'Hi ya.' Raj directed her greeting at Manjit with a sadistic twinkle in her eye. Her nonchalance laudable and adding to the spiralling mix. Manjit's breath momentarily being caught in his throat 'you okay…R…'R.' His strength had evaporated, deserted him, his legs folded and sphincter slowly loosening and letting out a carpet hugging fart.

'I think you mean Raj.' Kully slapped him on the arm confused by her husband's inability to string a sentence together. Hardeep similarly looked across curiously to the stumbling, blundering words stuttering out of his mouth. His body language was awkward and ashamed.

She stood there talking to him with all the innocence of a dominatrix, did they not realise that only several hours before he had his brothers wife on her back groaning with pleasure, stockings hanging off one ankle and her legs in the air as he passionately seduced her and sent her to ecstasy.

After the usual conversational pleasantries were further exchanged, the girls toddled off to the kitchen whilst the brothers caught up for a much needed *'gup shup' (chat)* in the main room. The succulent waft of Kully's home made curry teasing and tantalising their taste buds as they drank and chatted fervently covering a wide variety of subjects, including the tickets they had for the forthcoming football match in Liverpool on Sunday.

Although this particular evening was a great catch up session for the girls, it was fair to say that there had been a number of occasions where Kully and Raj had been at logger heads whilst they were growing up. This was partly down to Raj's pit-bull type and blinkered approach to most situations and arguments that they found themselves.

Kully was also a determined brute in many ways with her ability to detect cods wallop at five paces. Her bold and gregarious stance, often a defiant challenge for Raj, and anyone else for that matter.

Once these bulls locked horns there was always a dizzying cloud of mayhem and a barn storming verbal fracas that followed, with both of them refusing to back down. This was even the case in junior school such was their love, hate relationship and they had never grown out of it.

Despite all of this, the girls remained as close as was feasible in the given situation of being married to brothers despite the invariable cheat wagon having rolled on unpretentiously on one side for the past few months.

'So come on then how's your sex life?' Raj asked and striking with the deadly precision of a King Cobra. She sipped from her wine glass, the wine hitting the spot and warming her body nicely. The rim of the glass disguising her abominable smirk.

'Oh not great, we don't find the time as we used to.' Kully was open and transparent, the iron skillets of any kind of friendship. 'In saying that we are trying for a nipper now, so we have been trying.' Kully laughed and swigged from her wine glass too.

They chatted away whilst Hardeep emerged from the room and went upstairs to use the toilet. His thudding elephant feet could be heard rattling up the staircase.

Kully started to pour the leg chicken, sholay and gobi out into bowls along with the *'Punjabi viagra – a bowl of sumptuous green saag.'* She then placed a brimming and steaming bowl full of rice on the kitchen top along with a plate of roti for their delectation. Raj picked up the bowls and headed off into the living room/dining room where Manjit was sitting on his lonesome, still resembling a prisoner on death row with his open mouthed guppy like impersonation.

The adjoining wall that had originally separated the living and dining rooms had been smashed down to smithereens by the house's previous Indian occupiers. In an almost customary and religiously carried out tradition, a coach load of greasy haired freshies had been whisked in on the *'desi'* minimum wage of £1.50 per hour. They would work 23 hours a day, to knock the wall, and pave the way for one gargantuan room; and thus upholding the long held ritual recorded in the annals of history as being performed at least once in every Asian family's life time.

Raj walked through holding the dishes, her timing was impeccable as they were alone. She hastily placed the dishes on the table and seductively walked towards Manjit, she knew exactly what she wanted to do and chose her moment with aplomb. She glanced quickly over her shoulder and the coast was clear. He sat there afraid and full of self doubt, her lips flexing, pouting and very kissable. She was inches away from her prey as she hitched her skirt up to reveal the top of her suspender belt. She tugged the dress up a bit more whilst looking over her shoulder, the naughtiness and excitement lighting her up inside. She loved and thrived on the power she had at her disposal. He felt drawn to her, a magnetic pull mesmerising his soul and yet simultaneously gutting his innards like a piece of meat on a slab.

She stroked her own leg, vulpine like, moving her hand downwards slowly and with nefarious intent. They had been alone many times before but under wholly different circumstances. Her hand then began to travel upwards still very much attached to her silky suspendered leg, slipping away into the murky abyss of her inner thigh and under her dress. She looked down at Manjit as he lay on his back, his feet and legs bent and up in the air, his slobbering dog tongue hanging out of the side of his mouth and his tail wagging uncontrollably. In all honesty he may as well have been such was the excitement and sexual frustration building up inside of him waiting to erupt like a controlled explosion.

She then heard the elephant feet of her husband trampling down the stairs unsettling her style, the roaring of his trunk and chaffing of his tusks rattling the house, He had packed on a few pounds since they had married. Similarly, the wedding picture of Manjit and Kully hanging on the wall, nestling behind his former mistress snapping him back to reality like a bolt of electricity.

He flipped out his mobile, his hand jittery and shaking, placing it to his ear and speaking to his friend 'the invisible man'. He persuasively continued this fake conversation. Raj, meanwhile let go of the fabric of her dress and walked back into the kitchen. She could feel his eyes brimming with lust and following her as she walked gracefully across the room. Guys were like putty, she had once told a friend '*easily pliable,*' meanwhile Hardeep walked back in as Raj slinked off back into the kitchen, the foundations of her work for the evening laid out with the main course about to be served. How would Manjit extricate himself from the quicksand his very own living room was becoming? He wished he had stayed faithful to his wife. This was his biggest regret.

A few moments later, and dinner was served with the patrons sat comfortably, or not, at the dining table. Raj had somehow expertly orchestrated the seating arrangements so that she was sitting opposite her quarry and within touching range, whilst the other pair were blissfully unaware as they sat next to them indulging in meaningless and humdrum chit chat. As the four of them settled down into what was rapidly becoming *'the last roti,'* the fun had only just began.

The food was chomped, devoured and eaten with glee and the conversation was pleasant. At this stage, Raj managed to slip her shoes off and secretly snaked her foot under the table and across to touch Manjit's leg. Her foot travelled upwards until she reached his crotch. There it remained for at least five minutes as she prodded and poked, as well as massaged his fleshy thighs, jolting him with every deliberate prod and nudge.

Kully and Hardeep sat inches away from their loving partners blissfully unaware of the sexual tension and deceit being played right under their noses. After she was done, the foot came back down and back into her shoe. Her eyes screwed up as she caught Manjit's stare. A pestiferous look that exuded the warmth of a Rottweiler on acid, a glare of pure disgust as she looked on pitifully at the cretin sat in front of her; an author of his own misfortune she had assessed. The fun was over and it was as if something had snapped in her brain. She now wanted to play dirty, and Manjit could sense this from the look she had given him.

Shortly after dinner was over, Kully served a chocolate gateaux as dessert. This was polished off without quibble and they all lounged around in the living room. The time 10pm. It was agreed that the night would end early as they were all due to meet in the next two evenings with Hardeep's birthday and the pre planned girls/boys night. Manjit went to go to the toilet. Meanwhile Raj made an excuse to get herself another drink.

A few moments later after Manjit had composed himself in the bathroom, studying his reflection in the mirror and praying for the evening to conclude. He came out and headed towards the top of the stairs. When suddenly like a scene out of The Omen when one of Damian's satanic apostles emerges from the shadows. Raj started slowly walking towards him, a look of pure evil stretching across her face.

She walked out of the darkness directly up to his startled face, uncompromising and menacing. An anger personified and vengeance motivated look that would have turned most folk to stone. It was clear that this bunny boiling psychopath was a sophisticated but demented creature hell bent on destroying his very existence. Her necessity to slake her thirst in seeing his marriage crumbling like ash around her feet, and to further compound his guilt and betrayal before her very eyes seemed amongst the motivating factors edging this jezebel forwards.

Manjit stared open mouthed, what if someone saw them, surely she did not expect him to take her right here and now on the banister. Her voyeuristic tendencies beginning to make his sphincter twitch out of control.

He edged back against the wall. How long had she been waiting for him he thought painfully? His heels touching the wall, there was no more room for him to escape and the mood was decidedly bleak.

No sooner had he seen his life flash before his very eyes he blinked and she was on top of him, well almost. She was a whisker away from the very depths of his soul, his heart tossing around like a ball in a National Lottery machine. She was as unpredictable as a tornado as she glared at him through the narrow slits her eyes had become.

'So you think it is that easy to walk away from me do you?' Her voice menacing and his eyes flickering and closing slowly, laced with deep rooted fear. 'I...I...don't think this is a good idea...' he whispered in dread, his body caked in cold sweat.

Downstairs Kully and Hardeep made small talk whilst the storm continued to brew only a few feet above their heads. Kully stood up 'do you want some more gateaux?' she asked Hardeep. 'No, I am stuffed' came back the reply. Hardeep holding his belly with both hands.

She then walked into the kitchen area, seeking out another small slice of gateaux, the first piece not quite cutting the mustard for her. The gateaux sat on the bench enticing and seducing her into its slippery grasp, like a dripping plate of fat smiling back at her satisfying its sick lust to snare another victim. There were no signs of her friend or husband, she looked around and then into the hallway from her position within the kitchen.

'Manj you up there?' she enquired, perturbed by his disappearing act. 'Yeah he is in the toilet I am just waiting for him,' came back the immediate response from a cunning Raj.

Manjit could do nothing but look over his mistress shoulder as she stood there like a gargantuan dam and thus preventing any means of him burrowing his way out of the cess pit he had found himself in.

Kully placed her plate down next to the gateaux and went to grab the knife she had originally used to cut it, but it had disappeared, grown little legs and escaped into the sunset. She searched in the sink, on the floor and everywhere, but it was gone like a puff of smoke. Meanwhile upstairs the terror just cranked up a notch as Manjit who had now clearly had enough of being pushed around and harassed by her, went to push past Raj. Suddenly he was pushed back, her hand thudding into his sternum and careering him flat against the wall once again. It was then, through the cloud of darkness that he felt the sharp point of the large kitchen knife in his groin. The missing knife was in the hands of a possessed and demented killer. She smiled at him knowingly and it was surreal, here he was about to die in his own castle. It was just a matter of seconds before it was over and he knew it.

The knife was pressed deeper into his groin with Manjit resisting the temptation to whine like a puppy.

'What are you doing?' he whimpered. His spirit left his body and hovered above him for a second as his teeth began to chatter and shudder uncontrollably.

Raj's face resembling the yin yang symbol with the darkness slashing diagonally across her lower face and the other diagonal with the faint lick of the downstairs hallway light across it snarled back 'you used me you kuta.' Her voice mustering up all the hostility and abhorrence in that one sentence. There was a violent fury imprinted on her face.

One sudden move or nervous twitch would have brought on dire consequences for him, after all he had heard the stories about the ex girlfriend taking a pair of shears to her cheating boyfriend and then posting his piece first class to the poor guys mistress. At least Raj would be saving on postage as she could have practically tossed the fledgling member down the stairs and towards the entrance to the living room if she hankered such thoughts.

With these painful images whirring in his mind he stood like a statue and was on course to beat the world record for holding his breath, he had been already going strong for 30 seconds or so since he felt the death blade nestling all too comfortably next to his crown jewels. His motivation was to escape this incident unscathed, ghoulies and life intact in equal measure. He loved Kully dearly and did not want to lose her to a few months of infidelity, moments of sheer madness. It was wrong but to date no-one had invented a time machine, a device to turn the clock back, and therefore his indiscretions were stamped on his CV for eternity, that was a fait accompli despite his pining for redemption.

She felt the turbulence rising inside her. 'Are you going to tell her about us or am I?' she asked in voice that any would be serial killer would have been proud of.

He prayed for harmony, a conclusion to the madness he was confronted with when all he wanted to do was go downstairs for a slice of succulent chocolate gateaux.

His face now drizzled with sweat, his armpits gushing like garden hoses and his todger being read its last rites down below.

'I have got a good mind to cut your...' She stopped mid sentence and pulled the knife back as she heard the voice of her husband as he talked on his mobile phone out in the kitchen. She then rolled her eyes and cast a look of contempt before turning to head down the stairs, the knife was quickly concealed in a towel that she scooped up in her hands that had been draped over the banister. She walked down the stairs whilst Manjit let out a huge sigh of utter relief. He picked up another towel to mop the sweat from his face from his brush with death. His breathing still erratic and skittish as he shook his head, stunned by the incident that almost had him trying on an angelic wing for size.

He then waited before following her downstairs re-alising that he was up against an unrelenting psy-chopath in the form of Raj. A pugnacious and soul de-stroying nemesis hell bent on watching him squirm at every turn. Raj walked towards her hubby who had his back turned to her talking quietly into his mobile. She swiftly ducked into the dining room undetected and lingered ominously by the door. She remained out of sight of both the unsuspecting Hardeep and Kully who was by now chomping on her second plate of gateaux on the sofa in the living room that she had cut with an-other knife.

Raj stood there, subtly lowering the towel draped knife in the corner just behind a cupboard so that it was completely hidden and out of sight. Her hubby whis-pered away on the phone, unaware that Raj was hover-ing close by. Who was he talking to she mused?

Manjit meanwhile had also crept downstairs and walked up to the door, pausing when he saw her stand-ing at the entrance to the living room, the hideous and mortifying reality of his marriage lying firmly in the palm of her hand shaking and crushing his spirit like a sledgehammer.

He inched past her and into the living room, looking at her hands nervously. Her unpredictability and mental state the cause for his actions. He made it safely past the dragon and nervously walked up to Kully. 'Where you been?' she asked quizzically.

'I had a bit of diarrhoea.' He sat down quickly trying not to engage in any meaningful conversation whilst he tried to regain his already crest fallen composure.

Raj remained out of sight as she carried on eaves dropping. Hardeep finally terminated his call, his parting shot causing Raj's ears to stand to attention with sickening concentration 'right, speak later Gurpreet...and you take care okay, call you tomorrow.'

Gurpreet, who was that? The steam bellowing out of her ears as she shot into the living room so as not to arouse suspicion on her cheating spouse. Then again, she knew that she was not exactly the archetypal saint carrying on herself only that morning behind her husband's back. She sat down next to Kully whilst Hardeep entered the room clutching his phone in his hand. 'We have to make a move,' he said looking at Manjit. His voice peppered with a strange ebullience, no doubt because of the phone conversation with Gurpreet, male or female, they had made his evening just from the bewitched look on his face.

Raj stood up and said her goodbyes to Kully, hugging and kissing her on the cheek. She smiled and said goodbye to Manjit walking rapidly past his hunched shouldered and forlorn figure. Hardeep also performed the ritualistic round of goodbyes and the pair of them left. Hardeep suddenly stopped at the entrance and turned to

Manjit who was standing there soaked in guilt with Kully lingering near him like the invariable hang mans noose. 'Is everything okay geezer?' he asked his brother touching his arm with his hand.

Manjit forced himself to smile despite the urge to wail like a new born baby, 'yeah it is all good man.' His response easing and preventing the continuation of any further questions. Hardeep smiled and he and Raj said their goodbyes before departing. How long would Manjit be able to contain and suppress his dark secret from his wife and brother?

Manjit shut the door and turned to walk back inside. 'Did you notice something tonight?' asked Kully. Her question catching Manjit by surprise when all he wanted to do was relax and inspect the throbbing pain he was getting from his groin area where the knife had been pressed into.

'No what?' he responded hoping that she was not referring to the *'meeting'* that took place on top of the stairs.

'Well I don't think that I heard the pair of them talk once tonight, did you?

Kully's tone was inquisitive and accusing as she started to clear the dishes from the table.

Manjit looked up in thought. 'In fact I am certain that they did not exchange two words all evening, maybe they have had a fight or something' Kully added.

Kully continued with her surmising of the evening. It was a classic Indian foible that no sooner had your guests closed the front door, and even before they had even clunked their seat belts in their holders in their cars, the hosts would start rapaciously talking about them, gossiping as if their very lives depended on it.

This was the done thing and no sucker was a sacred cow when they had visited someone's house. The knives would be well and truly out, as the hosts would viciously dissect their every movement with a sadistic passion.

They say that gossip is the Devil's radio but this did not deter the ruthless hosts scattered around the country as each guest would be metaphorically ripped from limb to limb in the back biting post mortem and today Kully was in the mood to open a can of whoop ass on them much to Manjit's dismay. He made his excuses and retired for the evening whilst Kully tidied up. His thoughts tied up with the consequences of the last 3 months catching up and destroying his life. He walked upstairs feeling alone, concerned and bedevilled with guilt. How long would he be able to discourage his mistress from toppling him off the tight rope that he walked on so precariously?

Chapter 7

—⁓—

Sexy chica

Rita looked at the office clock hung on the wall, 5.15pm, and time to stop for the day. She normally finished at 5.30pm but for today, she was spent. The practice had been ticking over well and the usual office camaraderie had made the day go a lot quicker. Rita collected her shoulder bag and logged off her computer. It was Gaurav's turn to use the car today and as such he was due to arrive shortly to pick her up so she waited in the foyer with Amar. He always waited for Rita after work as the short walk to their cars, a quick drink after work were nice touches to polish the day off and consolidate their friendship.

As Amar and Rita talked, a blue Mercedes 190 car swept into the car park and parked in the far corner and nearest to the street. It was her hubby. 'Why the hell is he parking so far away?' she asked Amar, They both stared out of the window with baffled expressions.

The truth was revealed in shocking clarity when the passenger door was opened and a pretty young gori (English girl) got out and skipped off furtively into the adjacent alleyway leading into the main road. The car reverse lights then illuminated and the vehicle was reversed the entire length of the car park coming to a standstill near to the foyer of the solicitor's entrance.

It was obvious that Gaurav, the young dapper romeo, had not expected to be detected especially considering he had arrived 15 minutes early to pick up his wife. It appeared that sexual gratification outside of marriage was normal for this stud as he even plied his duplicitous trade under her very nose.

Rita was fuming and after holding back Amar who was at one stage pressed up against the window with his nose flattened and chomping to tackle her low life husband for her, she went to investigate herself. She flew out of the foyer and towards the parked Mercedes, the blaring bhangra music shaking the ground around where she was stampeding towards him on.

She yanked the door open and sat in, killing the music with a turn of the knob (that is the music dial and not the driver) the door still being held open. His cheating and dishonourable face was staring back at her complete with a cheesy smile. The look of cheap hotel sex plastered all across him, and further exemplifying his propensity to rebuff her erstwhile pleas to salvage their fragmented marriage from the jaws of defeat.

'What were you doing out there?' she asked without wasting any more time.

'Out where?' his response actually sounding genuine as he returned her stare unflinchingly.

'With that girl, who was she, a prostitute or mistress?' her voice incriminating.

Gaurav froze, his jaw dropping as the realisation dawned on him. He had been clocked and the tutti was careering into the fan in this cauldron of blight. It was evident from his goofy expression that he had not quite grasped the nettle of monogamy and hung on, as his trouser snake sought out adventures far afield then his bedroom. His actions lending themselves to an undoubted inexorable decline as the silence resonated within the car with Gaurav still dumb struck. She had just about had enough of the clutch of excuses that he had tried on her ever since they had tied the knot, and in the past few months where he had masqueraded as her husband.

Gaurav extolled the virtues and morals of an alley cat and looked on waiting for a reaction. He was not disappointed as he sat there waiting for the flame to reach the dynamite.

'You bastard,' she went to get out of the car 'how could you do that to me? There are some species of snakes out there with more integrity than you, get lost!' She screamed. Rita fought back the tears, he was not worth it, and in all honesty, this had been a regular occurrence over the course of their marriage. She had already shed enough tears over this kind of situation many times before.

Today there was no spillage of tears but just pure frustrated anger. As she went to slam the door shut he finally spoke up 'look she was just someone I met from school, that is all, why you taking this the crazy way again?'

She leaned back in once more 'do yourself a favour and go and think of a better and more plausible excuse and then try it on me, you might even raise a laugh, now piss off home.' She slammed the door shut with an almighty crash. Amar stared intently like an unblinking owl perched on a branch from his vantage position behind the solicitors windows. He continued to watch with quiet admiration. He had been like a crutch to her ever since she first talked about the problems she was having with her husband. Rita started to walk back towards him and came thundering through the door.

Rita stormed back in, her face flushed with anger, her fists clenched and teeth gritting. 'Arsehole!' she shouted launching her shoulder bag across the foyer and missing Amar by a pubic hair. She spoke deliberately and to the point. His fox brown eyes watching her intently and almost on the cusp of victory as she ranted on like Captain Caveman.

Although Gaurav and Amar had never seen one another, it was obvious from the stories that Rita had regaled Amar about her husband that he had grown an instant dislike to him and his womanising ways. Amar would sum up his hatred and discontent by adding zip to every occasion that Rita spoke ill of her husband, which happened to be virtually every time her relationship was in the spotlight.

He simply could not fathom how a girl like Rita was not worshipped or fully appreciated and that a slippery lizard like Gaurav was simply not worthy of having a princess like her. Incessant talk about foxes changing their hair but not their tricks punctuated the air for a few minutes as Rita tried in vain to calm herself down. Her idealism shattered in a whim after the latest incident.

'Look the bloke is an idiot and I just need to be away from him for a bit. Do you want to go for a bite to eat or something I just need to calm down here.' She paced up and down the foyer whilst Gaurav screeched off in his car in the background.

'Yeah no problems, I am in.' He offered her a cool and confident gaze.

'We will tell the others in case they ask what has happened that this, you and me going out for dinner and a drink is just a business meeting to discuss one of my cases okay? You know how gossip spreads.'

She sought to reassure her co-worker in simplistic terms that any hanky panky or other such frisky liaisons were strictly off limits and he concurred in a snap. All this wily predator needed was the time, space and presentable opportunity to work his magic, and the moment had just arrived trussed up on a silver platter.

Rita had a strong resolve and honed survival instincts, she was damned if she was going to play second fiddle to a string of play girls that Gaurav was frolicking with on a daily basis.

They waited for a few moments and then drove to a nearby restaurant serving a variety of culinary treats. The food and drinks were ordered and they chatted, Rita the most animated of the pair, her arms waving around as she expressed her frustrations and the inherent difficulties within her faltering marriage. This went on for the next 15 minutes until she began to calm down and then settle into a more relaxed mood with Amar, he had this soothing effect on her and she sensed this both physically and emotionally.

A little while later as they ate their food – the conversation dried up and the attraction between them increased tangibly. The two of them sat there in the silence and in the grip of sexual electricity. The chemistry that buzzes around when you know what you are both feeling and thinking. Rita twirled her spaghetti with her fork as Amar continued to stare at her. Amar was the first to stoke the fire 'look I don't want to wait another minute but you know I fancy the hell out of you. I want you bad.' He leaned in closer on the table in front of him, his arms relaxed and resting on the top.

'It is a risky game we are playing. I don't really want to be labelled as a cheater' her reply was full of regret. She continued 'you are not making this easy for me...' This was the first time Rita had admitted her feelings for Amar in a euphemistic manner. This was a revelation in their relationship that had just added the sprinkling of pizzazz to the cooking pot.

With the agility and quick thinking of a professional kabaddi player Amar exploited the situation and compliment 'yeah you know it chica.' Amar knew that his *'machee'* (fish) was toying with the bait and just seconds away from taking a chomp and being hooked on his lustful urges. Rita cogitated and then spoke 'he is about as useful as herpes, I mean who does he think I am? I am not worth what he is doing to me, why?'

Her words laced with disappointment and regret. She had tried for so long to mend his ways, to make him love her and cherish her but it was all to no avail as he failed to curb his enthusiasm of trying out other samples from her species.

Amar reached out and squeezed her thigh under the table, his passionate and all embracing grip sent a shock through her body, and she jolted back in her seat. It was all the reassurance that she needed to escape the train wreck that her marriage was becoming. The mere touch sent pleasures fizzing around her body that she had never felt.

'Ahh, don't do that here, someone will see. Remember you are just a work colleague and this is a business meeting for us to discuss my case remember,' she smirked naughtily, knowing full well the words held neither conviction nor a shred of truth. She was a willing conscript as her body ached for her lover to touch her body again just so she could feel his tremendously powerful passion an intent oozing out of his masculine body. 'So why don't you just ditch your husband of yours and come and live with me? I will treat you like a rani. I promise you will never want for anything ever again. I want your body that bad.'

Rita felt alive, wanted and resisted the urge to fall into her lover's arms like a love struck teenager. She knew that she had responsibilities, the need to keep her marriage alive, to rekindle the spirit and verve she had when she embarked upon the pit fallen road of marriage with her husband Gaurav. It was a futile and soul destroying exercise but typified her commitment and loyalty to try and recapture the spirit and love they shared when they first married. The goodness in her truly believed that this was attainable with effort from both of them.

However all said and done she loved the way that Amar made her feel about herself, his sweet intoxicating words edifying for her soul. He treated her special, listened to her, and above all was always looking at her with a hungry look in his eyes, a look that clearly stated that he wanted to ravish her at any given opportunity, in the filing room at work, the hotel on the way home, the back of the car – anywhere and everywhere.

Rita knew this, and even Amar knew that their urges were like a volcano of swirling and passionate temptation waiting to erupt at any given moment.

Even on his first day when they first clasped eyes on one another, when he started as a trainee solicitor. She had walked past him in a short black skirt, her long legs, curvy and voluptuous. 'Sorry but I have to say that you have the sweetest legs, I mean ever.'

She was taken aback by his confidence, but took it in her stride and commented back at him 'thanks, you look nice too,' she blushed and continued walking past, Amar studied her every inch of the way whilst beaming with a huge smile. He knew that all he had to do was play it steady, charm her, compliment her and he was in with a chance. He had gained a bachelors degree in seduction techniques over the years, as a consummate master of flattery, as girl after unsuspecting girl fell for his boyish charm, rugged good looks, and athletic muscular physique, not to mention the ace up his sleeve, his bad boy charm. Some girls are drawn to the violent rough and ready types like moths to a flame. The days of the smooth Milk Tray man were long gone, unless he had raped, pillaged and assaulted his way en route to delivering the chocs. The raping aside and Rita was definitely succumbing to his charm day by day.

He done what any experienced predator in the same situation would do, he ignored the wedding ring on her finger, he ignored all the token affection she had showed for her husband during the myriad discussions that they would have on their coffee breaks in the early fencing days. Above all Amar was always the first to swoop in with a caressing arm around her shoulder following on from the aftermath of an argument she had the day previously with her husband. This was the ultimate stealth tool to win her affection and he knew it.

This way he could throw in the compliments; his unique tried and tested humour, his caring side, and be all the things that her husband was not. All day and every day in the office he studied her, watched her, stalked her, drank with her after work to help distress from the office politics, the parties, the intimate probing of her relationship piece by piece like a jigsaw, all the time successfully plotting the downfall of her marriage.

He was an office coyote, and they say you should never underestimate the sexual desires of a work colleague like him. In every office up and down the country, there are guys like Amar waiting to exploit unsuspecting wives like Rita, by any means. The ring on the finger, pah, what does that matter? It is just another obstacle to overcome, another challenge, and another hunter winning the thrill of the chase.

Dinner was over, the drinks consumed and food finished off. The waiter produced the bill, which was paid off in a whim by Amar with Rita's pleading to contribute suitably batted off by him. They walked outside and back into his car exchanging a long lingering look across the roof before settling in inside. The tension was now palpable and deeply exciting. Amar sat in the driver's seat and Rita comfortably in the passenger seat.

Amar placed the key in the ignition and looked across. Rita was drunk on him, he was everything Gaurav was not, and above all, he wanted her badly. Her heart thumping wildly against her chest, the magnetism drawing them closer and closer when Amar leaned across to her from the driver's seat. His lips hovered close to hers before they met for a second; he kissed her tenderly trying desperately to suppress his volcano like passion within him from erupting. She kissed back for a second. It was heaven! She loved it. All of a sudden she moved her head back 'no, no Amar, I can't do this, I can't...I...am a married woman, it is not right.'

The uncomfortable and awkwardness of the moment rapidly started to fill the air around them within seconds.

With that she got out of the car 'look I will see you at work tomorrow, this never happened okay, let me get a taxi.'

Amar forcefully grabbed her arm to prevent her from alighting the vehicle 'hey, it is okay.'

He managed to then gently ease her back into the car 'let me drop you around the corner from your flat, don't leave it like this, we can talk about it on the way.' His words made sense and Rita closed the door pulling her leg that was trailing outside back in.

Amar set off with Rita looking out of the passenger window throughout the short journey. She got out of the vehicle around the corner from her flat, closing the door behind her without uttering a word. She felt utterly disgusted in herself for lowering her usually impenetrable defences and allowing the kiss to take place. Their relationship had just gone to a new level and there was every chance that the damage had now been done without a glimmer of recovery.

Amar drove off fully analysing what had just happened and licking his lips, the sweet taste of a peach driving his senses wild, after all, he had just tasted his own '*Hindu Punjabi forbidden fruit.*'

CHAPTER 8

—॰॰॰—

Catching up

Tejinder called Kully that evening just after she had prepared Saty's evening meal. She left him downstairs in front of the box as he attacked his heaping plate of sausage, mash and beans with satisfying glee. Before going upstairs, she stood at the entrance to the lounge and watched him devour the contents on his plate with the voracity, rapaciousness and speed that any Afghan hound or long haired Alaskan malmute would have been proud. She then walked out, her eyes lost in thought, her mind elsewhere and possibly with someone else, only she held the key to this labyrinth of knowledge.

Tej sat on the edge of the king size bed in the master bedroom, temporarily casting to one side thoughts of her Chewbacca husband with his hirsute snout in his plate downstairs. She sat for a few moments staring at herself in the dressing table mirror in the largest of the four bedrooms in her palatial des res. She picked up a brush from the dressing table and ran the bristles through her silky black hair. She reached over and flipped open her mobile phone. She called her long standing friend. They had known each other since those green days when they went through nursery and primary school.

They temporarily lost touch for a number of years when Tejinder's parents were forced to move to the Midlands due to her father's company shifting it's entire workforce and factory up the M1. Tejinder had always retained her good friend's details the moment she set foot back on terra firma in London. Kully was the first person she called announcing her return.

Kully picked up right away 'hey sweetie what's happening?' 'Oh nothing really.' I have just put some dinner on for Saty and thought that I would give you a call to see how you are.'

'Yeah I am okay, just relaxing.' I had a day off from work yesterday and today was a bit of a catch up with my in tray balancing precariously at one stage like the Leaning Tower of Pisa with bundles of accountancy paperwork.' Kully's voice sounding jaded.

'Ahh you poor thing, get Manj to give you a massage when he gets in from work.'

'Yeah that would be heaven wouldn't it.'

'I know, ahhh.' Well I just wanted to confirm that you are still up for the girlie evening on Saturday around here?'

'Oh yeah, don't worry that has been penned into the diary for ages.' I need to let my hair down with a few glasses of whatever. All this stress builds up doesn't it?' Kully stifled her yawn, the heavy day at work adding to her torpid physical and emotional state.

'Okay my darling, look there is something else, I need to talk to you about...it is just that well it is to do with me and Saty.' Tej walked over and closed the bedroom door and away from the potential prying ears from her husband downstairs. With the door closed, she continued 'I want to confide in you because I trust you, okay. I haven't told anyone else about this and please reassure me that your lips are sealed, I feel so bad saying this but I need to know you will take what I am going to tell you to the grave with you, okay.'

Her voice was sounding more and more serious and curt as she went on. Kully pressed the receiver closer to her ear and listened intently. What was the dark secret that was about to be unveiled? The earth shattering confession that her friend was about to unleash on Kully's already heavily weary and tired shoulders. Tej paused 'well, we are having problems…'

'What you are joking! No way!' Kully's eyes widened from the shock of hearing this news. There marriage was perfect, how could they be having problems? This and many other questions were racing through her mind as she tried in vain to fathom the confession her friend had made.

'Yeah it's true and I have been…' Tej paused for a second as she placed the hair brush on the bed, her ears fixed and tuned in towards the door.

'You have been what?' Kully asked anxiously. The scene almost like a classic slasher movie, whereby the victim doesn't get to finish the end of her sentence as the maniac slits her throat or cuts her gizzard out with a pair of pliers, all the time whilst her hapless soon to be next victim listens in on the other end of the line.

Kully asked again after having thought about her response for a moment 'are you having an affair?' She came out with what was by now becoming as obvious from Tej's furtive actions and responses as Saty landing the role of Cheetah in the latest Tarzan film.

Tej remained quiet, her eyes still fixed on the door, her breathing becoming more and more rapid. Her face scrunched up in trepidation. Then she heard her husband's paws galloping up the stairs. 'Look, I have to go...we will talk later okay...'

'Wait, just tell me are you seeing someone else, seriously are you?' Kully wanted to satiate her ever burgeoning curiosity before placing the receiver down.

'I have to go.' Tej went to press the end call button when Kully got one last question in at the eleventh hour 'how about lunch tomorrow, I will come and see you.'

Tej continued to whisper into her mobile as Saty was heard shuffling around in the toilet immediately adjacent to the master bedroom. She was aware that the walls were paper thin and every twitch could be detected without quibble. She cupped her hand over the speaker of the phone as she spoke 'I can't do tomorrow, I have...err...a busy day at work...err...look darling just forget I said anything.'

'Hey?' Kully responded bemused with Tej's discursiveness.

'Seriously forget it. I will tell you when I am ready...'

'Come on tomorrow, you can talk to me...' her face a smudge of approval.

'NO! Not tomorrow...see you Saturday okay, I have to go.' With that Tej hit the end call button and threw the phone on the bed. She held her head in her hands for a moment when she heard the flush of the toilet. She stood up and prepared to go to bed. Several moments later both Saty and Tej were asleep in their beds with their imaginations drifting off and clutching on to a multitude of thoughts so different to one another.

Meanwhile over at Kully's house a feverish conversation was taking place between Manjit and Kully over the gripping phone call that she had received. 'I am telling you she is over the side with someone; she practically spelt it out for me.' Kully announced, searching Manjit's face for some reciprocated enthusiasm at this latest scoop. Manjit sat on the sofa having returned from work a few hours earlier listening awkwardly to her ramblings. He chipped in with the odd grunt and sneering comment at the right times just to give the impression that he was actually vaguely interested in her scoop. His mind was preoccupied with something else. He looked disturbed and unsettled. A storm was brewing as he continued to sit like a curled up sloth on the sofa.

However, Kully was too embroiled in her friend's confession to notice and gossiped away. Why had Tej been so reluctant to meet her for lunch tomorrow especially when the coast was clear? There was something rotten and stinking about this and Kully needed to off load her suspicions on the one person she could rely on. She trusted Manjit implicitly and despite the assurances she had given her friend over the phone that she would not say anything. She knew this rule did not apply to her husband, after all they told each other everything (well almost…).

She was merely following the golden rule that when someone tells you something in confidence and makes you swear not to say anything to anyone, everyone tells at least one person, guaranteed. This is because everyone has at least one confidant, a tried and trusted soul to whom they will share any 'secret' with. In this way, the person who you tell will also tell the one person they trust, and if it isn't you, then the rule dictates that everyone in the close circle of trust will get to find out regardless.

The difference being that everyone is sworn to secrecy and therefore the original source of the information would be the dummy as all those around that originating person would know the secret that they think that nobody knows; therefore leaving plenty of scope for cheeky and tricky questions as they watch you squirm and conceal the truth.

The more Kully sank her fangs into Tej's infidelity, the more Manjit's position was tangibly weakening from his own exploits. He sat almost motionless and resembling a drenched rat pretending to channel surf through the cables on TV, all the time squirming every time Kully mentioned the word '*affair*' in the proceedings.

'So what do you think about her having an affair?' Kully kept on pressing the buttons, kept stoking the logs on the fire with her poker much to Manjit's increasing dismay. Which part of I can't talk about it because I am a surreptitious cheater myself did she not understand thought Manjit as he pressed the remote control buttons with increasing fury.

Kully satisfied that she had oozed every last droplet of conversation out of her beleaguered hubby then got up and went upstairs to retire for the evening. She kissed Manjit on the lips, a quick peck and she trotted off to bed. Manjit watched her leave and then took his mobile phone out. There was still one pertinent call that he had to make this evening, something that had shocked him on his journey home from work earlier that evening. He had to make sure his missus was out of the way, as this conversation was damaging to say the least.

He searched for the number he needed and pressed call. He sat back on the sofa waiting for the phone to be answered.

'Hey bro, kidda, you okay yeah, sorry to call you so late but I had to ask you something.' Manjit knew Hardeep would be up, besides it was only just after 10pm.

'Yeah cool, what's up?' Hardeep was sat in his study casually surfing the internet.

'I saw you today at '*Rocking Singh's Coffee Shop*' when I was coming back from work, who was that with you?'

Hardeep sat up in his chair, pushing the mouse of the computer away across the desk. His reactions with an air of anxiety around them. 'Where?' What you talking about?' His response jittery and lacking any composure. His dribbled response was lapped up with ease from a honed and seasoned liar that Manjit had been forced to become during those fiery 3 months of intense pleasure.

'I saw you with this Indian girl in the café, you were sat in the café by the window as I drove past. I don't know why I looked I just did and saw you both. Who is she?' Manjit was treading carefully knowing full well that he was the pot talking to the kettle.

'Nah wasn't me. I was at work.' Hardeep brushed off his brothers Agatha Christie questioning with his retort, hoping to move on to more trivial and unsuspecting matters.

Manjit laughed 'right so you were working at 7pm when I saw you, hey?'

'Fuck off. It wasn't me okay bhanchod, what you saying?' Hardeep had always had a nasty temper when probed and was nicknamed head butt Hardy when he was younger due to his penchant for nutting an enemy in a fight when the red mist began to descend. His temper was rising from his brother's insolent questioning, he had rumbled the reason for his sudden desire to *'work overtime'* so frequently of late and was not impressed as the net began to close in on him.

Manjit sensed that Hardeep had smelt the blood in the water and backed off 'oh yeah, must have been someone who looks like you. That's cool, sorry, anyway I better go. I will bell you tomorrow, it is your birthday in a couple of hours, feeling old?'

Hardeep sheathed the metaphorical dagger that he was holding and showed his first signs of relaxing 'yeah I know, anyway don't invent things cause it can cause trouble yeah.' He was seeking affirmation from Manjit. 'You haven't said anything about this guy you saw looking like me have you, I mean to Kully or anyone, have you?' His words desperate and searching.

'Nah, we don't talk like that.' Manjit capped off Hardeep's concerns with that one sentence and no sooner had they had this exchange, they said their farewells.

After Manjit placed the phone down, he smiled inadvertently. It was not as though he intentionally wanted to deceive his brother when he embarked upon his sordid affair with his wife; it was his fault, his weakness that he could not resist free sex when it was offered on a plate to him. It could have been from anyone.

This is one of the main reasons for affairs when the constant temptation is dangled in front of someone; the passes are made repeatedly, until that person succumbs. This is where the rot sets in. In the same way that most murders are committed by someone you know, most affairs are had by someone you know too. Ask yourself how many times would or could you resist the temptation if free, uncomplicated sex was offered to you by a sexy and gorgeous girl/guy...ponder on that for a moment! Everyone is human and everyone has needs, quick fixes, scratches that need a little tender loving itch every now and then...this is life!

The reason for Manjit's smile was obvious. He now had his brother in an awkward position if details of his relationship ever came out. After all, he was not the only one playing away from home; he was no doubt seeing someone else's wife also.

The girl he had seen was the kind of mature looking girlfriend who had married too early and was now after extra marital excitement as opposed to divorcing and causing shame to her family.

This was too-shay and honours even. Manjit traipsed up to his marital bed satisfied with this thought whilst Hardeep stared dejectedly at the computer screen, thumping his hand down on the table before getting up and heading off for bed, his thoughts in a whirl. The thought of his secret exposed and laid bare stripping the coated veneer around him with one chance sighting and one phone call. He lay down that night asphyxiated in despair and self loathing; he knew he had let himself down.

CHAPTER 9

—⁓—

Prisoner

Manjit flipped through the appointments folder, a pen held in place horizontally across his half open mouth. The fan continued to swish soothingly above his head on this balmy August Friday morning. His face concentrated carefully, his eyes scanning the names, addresses and notes scribbled in the diary section of the open folder depicting a swathe of monotonous visits stacked up one after the other. Manjit's shoulders heavy and drooping mirroring his mouth and soul as he judged how he was going to machete his way through the day. His other counterparts were not expected in for another half an hour or so. His brain pickled with these thoughts as he tossed the folder on to the table immediately in front of him in a petulant manner highlighting his anger at being stranded as the Lone Ranger.

His irritability causing the cup of coffee nestled invitingly on the table to go careering off to one side and skidding across the shiny desk surface, spilling its remnants mercilessly everywhere. The hot and steaming cup he had made only moments prior to being distracted with the mountainous workload in the folder, the frothy cup he had been desperate to help slake his thirst and elevate his mood.

'Ahh, you twat.' Manjit lifted the folder up to head level whilst simultaneously shaking it free from coffee. He threw the folder on his chair and searched for some tissues but there were none available. He walked to the back room and into the toilet, looking over his shoulder ensuring the shop floor was empty and devoid of any clinging vine customers hanging around with mindless intent. It was always quiet in the mornings, even the phones sat there silently staring back at him, stunned in silence, and seemingly smiling at his idiotic incompetence in spilling the caffeine shot.

He rolled the toilet paper around his hand from the loo roll until he had formed a huge pad around his entire hand before turning to go back into the stock room and heading towards the front office.

'You need a hand with that big boy?' A voice curtly chipped in. He looked up startled, wide eyed and brimming with fear, confronted by a silhouetted figure in the doorway, face disguised momentarily by the rays of sunshine shining through the office window. This was not the voice of his co-worker, his boss or any other ally or friend. Suddenly the figure inched to one side, hand resting firmly on the edge of the door frame and face like a shrivelled grape, twisted and contorted in a manner that would have made any championship winning gurner eternally proud. The hand on the door swiped quickly to one side slamming the door and escape route firmly shut with Manjit fixated to the spot like a deer in the headlights of a juggernaut. The fearless soldier then stepped forward some more, brash and soulless.

It was his old bed buddy Raj. She stood there smirking knowingly, one of her hands carefully concealed behind her back. What was she up to? What was she hiding? Manjit surveyed the situation as quickly as his brain would allow him, the shock of seeing her now dissipating slightly. Raj shuffled her concealed hand in quick succession behind her back.

This was bad, it appeared that she had come prepared to finish this episode for the final time, armed with a blade. The psycho had brought a knife to murder him in his workplace. He would be murdered shamefully by his jilted ex in ceremonious fashion, his body slumped in the toilets whilst incriminatingly clutching a roll of tissue papers; The headlines *'toilet wazzer meets his grizzly end at work.'*

'You are a tosser, thinking you can use me when it suited you…well who is laughing now? Now we'll see.'

'Raj, what are you…' his response stalled and misfiring, a man tortured by his past.

Raj stepped forward, she wanted her pound of flesh and here he was practically with the seasoning on his head. It seemed that she had a pathological desire to ruin his life as she fiddled with something behind her back.

Manjit's heart was pumping away furiously, his eyes focussed up and down between her scowling expression and then to the tool fidgeting behind her back, soon to be thrust into his throat.

The fear embalmed in his body as he stepped back tentatively, being careful not to make any sudden movements. He looked on anxiously and in heedlessness as she remained firmly ensconced in the path of his only means of escape, he was defenceless, unarmed and his only hopes of salvaging himself from this dilemma would be to wet the tissues and throw them at her, either that or to plunge dramatically to his knees, hands clasped asking for redemption. He stood there wallowing amid an ever spiralling and sweltering sea of acrimony and despair.

Raj deliberately kept her hand behind her back as the powder keg moment lingered for a few more moments.

'I am going to make you pay…Today I will give you a lasting memory, one that you won't just walk away from, you feel me…you saala.' The silence broken with her threatening and scornful words. She was going to scar him for life, the knife would be slashed across his face, she would cut his nuts off and leave them in the cat's tray on the way out. He was on the one way train to Doomsville without a return train ticket in sight.

He stood frozen to the spot, the fight had left him, spilled and dripping to the floor just like the cup of coffee. He accepted his fate, his karma was sealed and he involuntarily closed his eyes. He stood waiting for the stamp of fate in the form of the soon to be thrusting knife in his belly to hammer the final nail in his coffin and close this chapter once and for all. He had missed his opportunity to escape several minutes earlier when he first saw his nemesis appear. They say that when you are first confronted with danger, then all humans have the fight or flight mechanism in built in all of us with the adrenaline surging throughout our bodies.

However, the caveat being that if you wait any longer than a certain window of time then your fight WILL turn to flight. This is because the initial surge of adrenaline was there to prepare you to fight, with more strength that you would normally possess, such as miracle stories that we are regaled with whereby mothers have lifted cars to help their children escape being trapped and so on, and without a can of spinach in sight.

The problem being, if you let this strength wait, idle without use then that is when you get the shakes and jelly legs and it unequivocally means that your window of opportunity has evaporated. Thus, Manjit's inability to react in the early moments of the encounter had rumbled his survival chances and he therefore resigned himself to his fate.

Raj walked forward, moments away from ending their messy web of deceit, she stood inches in front of her prey, her hand slowly moving from around her body, aimed at his torso, unflinchingly accurate her hand appeared a whisker away from his quaking body. He looked on through squinted eyes, how he had once enjoyed being this close to his mistress and in the flames of passion rather than the icy jaws of defeat as he was right now. The death scythe lowering down over his head and casting a shadow of impending expiration.

All of sudden – BANG! Manjit flung himself back on the solitary desk propped up against the wall. His body sweaty and laced with a fear he had never felt and was unlikely to ever feel again. His hands instinctively clutched his torso as he lay there half on the desk and half hanging on the floor, his feet jumbled up in some kind of intricate Michael Jackson dance move. There was another momentary silence. He had always heard stories in the pub about when you were knifed and how it felt like a punch, or a heavy kick and never actually like you had been stabbed. He recounted this; he could not feel any sharp pain but knew that as soon as he saw the blood he would go in to shock. He opened his eyes slowly and looked down his body.

There was no sign of blood; he sat up a bit more, still looking terrified. He was convinced that he had been gutted like a fish, but again, nada, nothing. He looked up and saw Raj standing with her hand pressed firmly on a piece of paper, which she had slammed on to the desk. 'Read that,' she slid it over to him and stepped back. Manjit looked down at his torso and was relieved not to see copious amounts of blood drowning him, there was nothing just the sound of his knocking knees and sphincter allowing a nervous fart to seep through his bum cheeks.

Manjit slowly picked the letter up and inspected the contents. It was a letter from the local hospital; he read quickly trying to draw out the salient points as rapidly as he could muster. Then he saw the moment when his chutney well and truly slid off his samosa. It was there in black and white. He looked up at the letter head, it was authentic, and the signatures were all real. He stared again in total horror and disbelief: The letter was addressed to Rajinder Dhaliwal and the excerpt that hit him between the eyes like an arrow read;

'I can confirm that you have HIV...'

There was no need to read anymore. He looked up at Raj. She stood there impassive. She had received the letter that morning from the local hospital and had already come to terms with the results. Her appointments with the hospital over the last few months had culminated in this death sentence. 'He had destroyed his life, if she had Aids, then he must have contracted it too. His life was falling apart more than even he could have imagined. What about Kully?

'How?' He pleaded for some answers, any lucidity in his darkest hour.

'You tell me, you are the one who is sleeping around with all these girls behind your wife's back. I will never forgive you for what you have done. I have to live with his hanging over me and so do you now – you BASTARD!'

Raj screamed, her anger summed up in the word bastard. He had ruined both their lives. The root of the deadly virus was unknown, but in the moment irrelevant. Manjit had to get checked out and then have the soul destroying wait for the results. His life hung in the balance, his foundations crumbled to ashes. His desire to have kids eradicated with the single piece of paper he was left holding in his hand. He began to whimper, searching for answers. 'No, no this can't be happening.' His voice cracking.

She yanked the letter back out of his emasculated grip and turned around walking towards the other door. She opened the door and looked back at the hunched up and forlorn figure of the stud she once dreamt about and had seduced; she shook her head 'pathetic tosser.' She walked out of the office and disappeared leaving Manjit as a drippy sack of sorrow, guilt and fledgling self doubt. The wound was deep and unrecoverable and now both lives had been torn apart, two worlds had collided with life changing results driving stakes through any potential happiness they had once envisaged, all for a few nights of stolen passion...this was the roulette of life and they had rolled the dice and LOST – emphatically...

CHAPTER 10

—⁓—

Sub rosa

She looked at her watch; it was looking as grim and desperate as a hookers piss flap. She was running late. Rita had quickly popped home in her car, a short drive from the office. She had made this journey umpteen times in the past and never once made it back late to the office. This one time, however she was in extremis, as the traffic was snarling everywhere without any respite. Every which way she turned there was a traffic congestion. It was Friday morning and it seemed as though the world and his wife were out in force. Her frustration continued, her face reddening as she searched feverishly for a way out of the wallowing situation she found herself in. All she wanted to do was to circumvent the bottle necks of traffic that were appearing as if from nowhere and sit back comfortably behind her desk without arousing any suspicion from her boss.

She had been forced to return home this morning as she had forgot to scoop up her mobile phone that she had left on the kitchen table in her frantic rush to get to work earlier. She needed the phone to make a vital call from a stored number contained on the sim card memory.

All of a sudden she had the eureka moment where she would turn the car around and negotiate her way through the back roads and take the scenic route back to base. A satisfying glint appeared in her eyes as she swung the car around in the tiny side street much to the consternation to other road users. She then intricately performed a twenty three point turn, nudging and stealing an inch every manoeuvre. She eventually managed to obviate her predicament as she sped down the road away from the snarled up traffic and satisfied that she would be able to effectively machete her way through the side roads to destination office without too much kerfuffle.

The mobile phone contained the number of her grandma (naneeji) – YES you heard correctly, it belonged to her 84 year old, fully dentured up granny. Rita's parents were Hindu Punjabi, her mother being Sikh and father Hindu. She was very close to her naneeji and tried to call her every few days, especially now that she had full access to her 24/7 with her newfangled device.

The family had chipped in recently and brought naneeji Harbajan a Nokia pay as you go phone as a Christmas present. This way they planned she could stay in touch when she was out and about with the girls doing her '*thang*' in the local clubs complete with her fellow '*Naneeji's Girl's Aloud Band.*'

The family would tease her with their visions of her trussed up in the latest street garms. Her chunni (head scarf) still with the label hanging off it, her black bikers leather jacket, stone washed denim jeans. She would even have her white hair slicked back and held firmly in place with strong holding gel; the latest designer pumps, and not to mention arm swinging west side signs she would make at family functions.

However, despite the teasing and rib elbowing shenanigans the old dear's time was up as she faced the prospect of popping her clogs and sleeping in her casket for a long, long time. The ticker was weakening as the days rolled past and her expiry date was almost up. Rita wanted to phone her and see how she was doing and when she could go and visit her back in the family home in Bristol.

Still she had the phone in her possession now and just needed to get back to the office undetected.

The bosses were not overly enamoured with their staff using their vehicles during their lunch breaks for exactly the reasons that was causing Rita such anxiety as she swept across the urban roads like the Blue Flame in her Mercedes. She had the car for the day as Gaurav had taken the day off to run errands for his mum, or at least that was what he had fed Rita the previous evening.

Rita laughed as she turned into the road of her good friend Tej, a necessary deviation on her detour to the office. She whizzed down the road approaching the residence of Tej. In the distance she caught a glimpse of her four bedroom semi detached house sitting snugly between a couple of mock Tudor houses. The chimneys on either side, casting imposing figures in the skyline, a vista of cloud tufted peaks in the skyline. As she drew closer, she noticed a figure standing at the entrance to her house and searching the street both ways with frenetic shifting of his head. The figure, a middle aged Asian man, stubbly and donned in a black gangster overcoat, collars turned up, looking as shifty as Jack the Ripper in a brothel.

Rita eased her foot off the accelerator for a moment and let the car coast past without any assisting throttle.

She did not recognise him and from his actions he looked suspicious and up to something obviously nefarious, but she did not know what – yet!

Her car drew closer and she gently applied the brakes, slowing down to cast her beady eye over this imposter and trespasser on her friend's property. She knew that Saty was out as his red Honda Accord was missing from the drive and Tej was in all probability at work in her practice.

Just as Rita was about to slam on the anchors outside the house, roll over the bonnet of the car and scream 'freeze you son of a diseased testicle' she relented when she amazingly saw the front door of the house suddenly opened. Her heart stopped for a second, maybe this was a team of burglars and he was the look out. It all made sense. She cruised by slowly past the house slowly craning her neck to survey the situation. She parked up discreetly in a clear patch of space and watched hawk like through her rear view mirror, her mobile clutched in her hand ready for a call for assistance if needed.

The shifty collared guy smiled and nodded his head obviously engrossed in conversation with his henchmen doing the number within the house. All of a sudden – BANG! The shock wave shot through Rita's body. a small head poked out from the door frame and searched nervously down the street. The quick stealthy looks down both sides of the street were nervous and caked in deceit.

The body language clearly that of a malefactor. She squinted her eyes to make sure, but the floating head in the doorway was Tej. She saw her friend take hold of the arm of the shifty guy and pull him inside towards her. Her actions furtive and full of patent duplicity. She was seeing someone behind her husbands back, while he was out. Rita sat there for a moment trying to decipher exactly what she had seen, open jawed and in utter incredulity.

'Oh my god…' she whispered to herself. She had actually caught her cheating on her own doorstep with her fancy man; the rough looking Mafioso button man was her bit on the side whilst her hubby was blithely unaware. The strict fiscal rules of marriage shattered in the moment she invited the stranger into her arms, her life and her bed. She quickly snapped thoughts of them getting dirty and raunchy between the sheets out of her mind and concentrated smartly on her next objective of getting to the office and explaining why she was twenty minutes over her lunch break. She drove away pop eyed and her mind a state of confused perplexity. She understood why she would cheat on her hubby, maybe the 'wolf' didn't quite cut the mustard in the sack and this was merely physical release with no stings attached. An emotionless encounter, a throw away fling to simply satiate her need to be lusted over by her musky advocate.

Rita made it back to the office eventually but was relieved to see the bosses were out to lunch and she was in the safe zone. As she walked in Amar winked at her from his desk. Rita acknowledged and sat down by the landline phone on her desk, she toggled for a number on her phone, her naneeji's – NO, first she had to break the news to a friend in true Busby style.

'Hi, Kully can you talk?'

'Yeah what's up, you okay? You sound out of breath.' Kully responded slightly alarmed.

'Guess who is having an affair, go on guess?' Rita whispered with morbid excitement.

'I know, are you talking about…'

'TEJ.' they both said her name in unison and laughed feverishly, and not very friend like.

'How do you know?' asked Kully. Rita regaled the story to her in a 20 second sound bite.

Once Kully had heard this appraisal, she recited her phone conversation with Tej last night.

The pair of them nattered away for the next few minutes, exchanging their viewpoints and disapproval. After a short period, they stopped for air and agreed not to divulge anything to Tej or their other halves. They stuttered and spluttered as to whether they would spill the beans to Raj and decided that she deserved to know as she was a fully signed member of the *'The Hounslow Crew'* so she would be told when the timing was right.

Hardeep's birthday that evening was going to be interesting as the girls promised to pay delicate attention to every peccadillo and twitch that Tej made. The fun was just about to begin...

—~~—

CHAPTER 11

Lust

After an hour or so of working in the office with the phones constantly ringing, the fax machine crackling into life every other minute and the sound of the coffee percolator bubbling away temptingly in the background Rita had to retrieve some files held in their office archive filing cabinet in the office along the corridor. This was where the swingeing amounts of legal documentation were safely housed for future litigation. Her client a slightly obstreperous dame was being meddlesome in a call that Rita had just fielded, whereby she had requested full and concise details relating to her case. Rita had responded in her most dulcet and relaxed telephone manner promising to call her back within half an hour.

Rita was stood outside the door to the archive office. She swiped her card into the electronic card reader. She was inside within seconds and immediately began to fumble her way through the stacks of files and boxes, the door shutting slowly behind her. She had been in there for over 5 minutes sifting through the mountainous paperwork trying in vain to find her clients paperwork.

When suddenly she heard someone shuffling around outside. Then she heard the swipe card reader being swished. She turned to look, surprised and equally curious to see who the coincidental office worker was. The door was slowly pushed open and in entered the serendipitous soul.

Rita's expression remained unchanged but her heart began to beat like a dhol player on a combination of speed and an injection of several cans of Red Bull. Her hands were occupied with holding a box then suddenly began to feel clammy, her body murmuring with the tiniest of shivers and tingling sensations running amok inside her, swirling around her erogenous zones.

The subject of her arousal was none other than Amar. He stood there at the entrance silently stalking his girl, watching, teasing, tempting and studying her reactions. He was a player and he knew when the signs were good, when the green light was blinking and beckoning him over. They basked in one another's adoring and erotic eyes for a moment of intense rapture.

The door was now fully closed and he stepped closer towards her quaking body, the shivers in her hands making the box shake as she struggled in vain to keep it steady. Her breathing erratic and a tell tale sign of her intentions. He stepped within her personal zone, her breathing hot and bounding with temptation and imminent pleasure.

Amar could wait no more; this was his chance to show her exactly how much he needed her body. He took a firm hold of the filing box, tugging it out of her hands and throwing it to the floor. They stared into each others eyes; there was a connection between them. Physical, emotional and lust fuelled.

'What are you doi…?' Rita's response was cut short as Amar reached forward with his hand gripping the back of her head passionately and kissing her full on the lips. His other hand stretched out and running up her thigh and hoisting her leg to his side, her hold ups ripping slightly as he cupped his manly hand underneath. He pressed his body up against hers and pushed her back against the filing cabinets. Their senses lost in this erotic embrace as they kissed hard on the lips, letting the pent up frustrations of the months pour out in this single moment. The months of flirtatious behaviour, the teasing and complimentary comments had culminated in this fiery tryst of unbridled lust. Rita was now lost in a surreal, sepia tinted fantasy with her hunky, bad boy lover.

Then without warning, Rita suddenly pulled her head back. What had he done he thought with a concerned expression emblazoned across his face. 'No, no stop…I can't do this.' She sounded apologetic and guilty as she placed her leg back on the floor and quickly moved her body to one side from him. Amar eased back himself. He respected her and listened closely still baffled to her sudden change of heart.

'I am married, I can't do this, it is wrong. I had better go,' she straightened her skirt as it had been hitched up by Amar's searching hands and dabbed her fingers underneath her lips trying to patch up the lipstick that had smeared around her mouth. It seemed that her clout had been her saving grace in this fickle and fiery situation. Her face frowned in thought and guilt as she fidgeted next to him. He practically fell back on his haunches with a feeling of inner dejection and crushing defeat.

Amar stood in frustrated silence, glancing across at her shrewdly. He wanted her bad, not just for a quick fling but for keeps, and now she was walking away from him discarding his desires and hopes in a snip. Rita was a decent girl and knew that there was no way that she could carry on with an extra marital affair behind her husband's back. This was simply not her style, she was better than that and despite the burning attraction and sexual chemistry overcoming her, she wisely relented from letting the situation exacerbate any further than it had the potential of doing so.

She moved to the door and placed her hand around the door handle clinging on to the wispy thought that it was Amar, who had instigated the kiss; and that she was merely distracted for a sweeping lust filled, but special moment. Just as she was about to pull it open Amar jumped in front of her and shouted 'why are you being so loyal to that rat hey?' His question startling her pretty face and amplified with the acoustics in the tiny room. He continued his jaundiced comments 'would he stop if this was him, hmmm, no, he would-n't. I don't see what you see in that dead beat!' Amar shook his head 'he has played you for a fool since you got married, and the truth is he will never change, never – face it.' He shouted fiercely, turning and thumping the door with an open hand, letting out his anger and feelings towards his nemesis. His eyes full of hate and pour disgust for her husband, the look of a killer some would say…someone who would do any-thing to get what he wanted, including if someone in-terfered with his goals.

Rita stared at him open mouthed. She was strangely drawn to this rough and ready type of personality and he pressed her buttons. Her hand let go of the door handle and she listened intently.

'Are you prepared to put up with second best, well are you?' His question rhetorical. 'Nah, nah you are better than that maggot, I am telling you, he does not deserve you, no way.'

Amar motioned with his hand moving it side to side in front of his body, his face curled up in a ball of hate as the words swept out of his mouth without remorse. If Gaurav was within the radius of a mile of him then he would not have been responsible for his personified anger, he epitomised the look of a killer, someone who was covered from head to toe in red mist, walking jail bait.

Rita's eyes moved to the floor, unsure what to say or what to do. 'Leave him and be with me.' He moved closer 'I will love you like no other guy has ever loved anyone in their life. I promise. You will be my rani, my sweetheart, the girl I would die for, that is how much you mean to me. Just leave that cockroach first.'

'I can't...he is my husband.' Her words weak willed and lacking any conviction.'

Amar chipped in 'are you trying to convince me or yourself?'

She paused as she composed her reply 'you have to understand I have to make it work.' Amar rolled his eyes in disappointment, she seemed lost. 'I am going to look for another job; it will be too difficult to work alongside you anymore. Her voice pitiful and deflated.

Amar tried one last attempt to get her to see reason as he took hold of her hands in his. He looked into her eyes and into her soul as he spoke 'I want to spend the rest of my life with you and am prepared to do anything it takes, anything.' His words chilling and powerful. What did he mean? With that, he stepped forward and reached for the handle opening the door of the office. Rita wiped the trickle of tears that snaked their way slowly down her face with her fingers and walked out of the room and down the corridor back into the main office. She made a hasty excuse to Susan her co-worker, something about not feeling well and asked her to take on the job for the vociferous client who had phoned earlier, and was partly responsible for this mess.

Amar waited for a few moments and then returned slowly to his desk. His thoughts a medley of confusion, heartache and combined devastation. He searched the office for his beau, but she had gone, his *Hindu Punjabi Elvis* had left the building.

He was defeated and down trodden. His race was over and a life time of pining for his dream girl was the reality he faced. He picked up a pencil and twirled it in his hand as he concentrated on what had happened. The taste of her luscious lips still fresh, her perfume lingering on the collar of his shirt; suddenly he snapped the pencil in half and squinted his eyes. If he couldn't have her then what did life mean to him he mused.

His mind warped, his face cunning and predatory. All of a sudden he knew exactly what he had to do, he had hatched a plan in that moment, something that was going to change all their lives forever. He smirked with the evil thoughts festering…he predicted suffering for anyone connected to her…

CHAPTER 12

—〰—

Surprise

Meanwhile over at the estate agency a destitute and heart broken Manjit sat hunched over his desk. His head caressed in his hands, fingers gently stroking his own hair.

His heart heavy and soul battered from the bomb shell he had heard before.

This was a murky mess, a wake up call from hell. It meant that there was every potential that his death warrant had been signed on this very day. Being HIV positive in anyone's language meant the strong possibility of meeting a guaranteed sticky demise and it was only a matter of time. He was vaguely aware that there were drugs available for him to counter the spread of HIV, but he knew that he was now very much snared in this game of lottery as soon as his eyes had seen those damning words earlier.

HIV (human immunodeficiency virus) mainly affects and attacks the body's immune system and in particular the T cells, macrophages amongst other cells. This way the body becomes more prone to picking up rogue and opportunistic diseases and infections as more and more cells are picked off this way. Eventually the individual would then develop AIDS (acquired immunodeficiency syndrome) and in all probability snuff it, although there are drugs available to help manage and sustain the carrier. Manjit was now very much in this game of Punjabi roulette.

He flipped his wrist over and looked at the time, his eyes red and face flushed beetroot where it had been buried in his hands. Only a couple of hours before he had to leave the office, and return home to face his doting wife. He had been so naïve. so innocent. Why did he not use protection during their affair?

Why had he not read more carefully about the twisted world of STD's and other such internal afflictions? Most importantly, why had he not resisted her advances the very first time she made a pass at him that day in the house? Only he knew the answers to these questions as the reading of his epitaph lingered ever closer to his deflated carcass.

Life was cruel but the devil was in the detail. If you have an affair, then be prepared for the consequences. The odds were stacked against him; after all, he was sleeping with a girl who was HIV positive. So many questions and concerns cropped into his head as he cogitated further. How could he tell his brother? Did she do this intentionally? Did she know before?

The psychopath had snared him as she said she would, but he knew full well that he had played the game of chance of his own accord. He felt like crying as he thought about the impact this would have on his life should he also be a carrier. They say that when you sleep with someone unprotected then you are not only sleeping with that person, but all the people that they have ever slept with and the people who those partners have ever slept with and so on. This invariably increased your chances of contracting a disease of some description.

A disease silently waiting on the peripheries to pounce, engulf, and steal your liberty forever.

It seemed that essentially Raj in her sexual travels had picked up the fateful virus and was now the purveyor of death for Manjit amongst others.

Manjit took a swig from his cup of coffee. He had to straighten himself out before he saw his missus and especially as it was his brother's birthday party that evening. He took his mobile out and called a pre saved number.

'Hi, is that the doctor's surgery. Can I make an appointment at the earliest opportunity.' He waited for a few seconds 'the earliest you have is Monday morning.' He paused, it was the only option available. 'Okay, please book me in.' He passed on his name and terminated the call, safe in the knowledge that he only had the weekend to see through before he received his fate. In the grand scheme of things, it was only a few days and he would know either way. He went to put the phone back on the desk when his message alert vibrated on the mobile.

He opened the message and read it to himself. He immediately felt nauseous. It was the kuti again; she was a professional stalker and intent on ripping his heart out and serving it on a plate to him. The message disembowelling him momentarily and adding to his deepening sense of gloom;

'When are you telling Kully about the filthy disease you have given me – you fucking low life?' You had better tell her or I WILL!

Like a classic Bollywood film, Manjit could see a picture of Raj floating in the middle of the text message as he read it out in his mind. After he finished reading it the floating face disappeared with a puff, as did Manjit's ability to stop his sphincter from holding back the brown headed turtle warrior that was slowly beginning to protrude into his underpants and enter the big wide world. He clenched his butt and quickly made his way to the staff toilet stuffing the phone in his pocket before he really did shit his pants.

He sat on the cold rim of the toilet and defecated like a trooper, pebble dashing the inner bowl like a machine gun. His thoughts were a jumbled up composite of fear and anger as he continued praying for the weekend to pass and for the appointment on Monday.

He just wanted to seek solace in the sanctum of the doctor's surgery. He needed to talk to someone, with his wife was not even an option, his brother would be a suicidal move and Raj was as mad as a box of snapping turtles.

He felt it best not to involve anyone in his dilemma including his trusted friend Saty and just wanted to deal with the issue on his own until he received confirmation either way. His secret was confidential and he wanted to lock it away in the darkest depths of his mind and heart. He strategized how he would merely put on a brave face that evening and the other get together on Saturday night. This was easy as he was used to covering up and lying as he had done so successfully during his duplicitous affair. This situation was nevertheless eating away at him and sapping all of his mental strength.

Manjit had finished on the toilet and with his mind in turmoil he reached behind him instinctively, his hand searching for the empty milk bottle he could use to wash his arse with, the one he had used throughout this child-hood. It was normally the one with the brown residue around the rim and congealed pube stuck to the side.

He snapped himself together, what was he thinking? There was no bottle at his workplace, his mind confused and twisted with worry. It was clear that he was not thinking straight but it was hard to take some little foibles out of his frame of reference. He stood up and walked back out after cleaning up. How would Raj react when she saw him at Hardeep's birthday?

The evening had disaster, divorce and time bomb plas-tered all over it and there was only a few hours to go before he entered this snake pit of hostility...even the clicking of his ruby slippers was not going to extricate him from the cauldron of despair awaiting him. He mumbled God's name under his breath and prayed for some kind of resolution as the clock ticked towards his destiny...

CHAPTER 13

—🔊—

Truth or dare

Friday evening at Raj and Hardeep's house and all four couples sat around the living room, on the couch, on puff bags on the floor, on the dining room chairs that had been moved in to accommodate everyone. In the centre of the room lines of wine bottles, whiskies, rum and vodka all lined up, some erect others empty and toppled to their side portraying a fine festive display of alcohol being enjoyed by all. They had been drinking for three hours with all manner of concoctions being consumed.

All throughout Manjit kept looking across at Raj, not sure which way she would turn that evening. Despite drinking Bacardi after Bacardi he was on tenterhooks and staying alert to the possibility of her making a grandiose confession to mark the occasion, just like the turncoat she was. Hardeep, rapped his knuckles on the coffee table in the centre of the room capturing everyone's attention 'okay folks, let's have some fun, then, get this show rocking! His voice showing the eagerness of someone keen to raise the stakes in the group's interaction.

On this cue and suitably fuelled by booze, Gaurav leapt off the sofa and started to grate his hips in the middle of the room, the oodles of rum in his system assisting his Punjabi salsa/Elvis Singh snake hip jiggling routine as the group clapped and cheered vociferously. His dancing becoming morefeverish and raucous with the animated and *patti'* group egging him on like demented seals.

He gripped the collar of his sweatshirt and pulled his top over his head revealing a granite like ripped six pack, along with bulging pecks, and proper man sized biceps, those babies were mini rockets as he would purr consistently to the bits of crumpet who have been enticed in his come to bed spell.

The girls, Kully, Raj, Tej began wolf whistling and falling about laughing and nudging each other, the guys Saty, Manjit and Hardeep tapping the tables with their hands and cheering him on in the impromptu drunken frenzy. The HIV issue seemingly brushed under the carpet by Raj, who by being tanked up on alcohol was revelling in the moment and celebrating large with the girls. Similarly, Manjit had seemed to put his problems aside as he roared on with the lads. All the while Rita looked on poker faced and seemingly deplored by the antics of her stage performing hubby.

Amidst the chaos and as Gaurav placed one foot on the glass coffee table amongst the strewn bottles of booze, Hardeep glanced across and immediately sensed the palpable tension and infuriated glare that Rita was transmitting and shouted 'okay that's enough bro, let's settle down, I have a better game'. The raucous crescendo slowed down and Rita gave Hardeep an acknowledging look with her eyes, a thank you for having the wits about him to decipher the mood. Raj never once took her eyes of Gaurav's six pack, her thoughts spinning with visions of her hands starting from the top two six pack muscles and then slowly travelling south until they reached the groove between the lower muscles. She was almost salivating at the thought, her HIV not registering for one iota as a red flag.

Manjit meanwhile looked at Raj as Gaurav was putting his sweatshirt back on, he too noticed her eyes transfixed like a magnet to the rippling physique being dangled like a juicy carrot in front of the nymphomaniac. She had once told Manjit in one of their frequent sex fuelled sessions that she went weak at the knees when a guy had a good, toned flat stomach and meaty pumped up footballer legs. The sort of nut cracking thighs that she could bite, nibble and suck, and Gaurav's thighs were as thunderous as they came. Raj looked back at Manjit and smirked knowingly, teasingly as she sat opposite him. It did not matter; the look had not even registered with him. He had already renounced the sordid life of murky affairs as long as she was acquiescent with this reticence.

Gaurav went to sit down, Raj sensed Manjit still looking at him and crossed and uncrossed her legs discreetly, revealing a pair of silky red knickers. Manjit saw them and was a whisker away from a full cardiac. It was surreal as she would normally flounce around commando and this was a torturous gesture if ever there was one. He quickly looked away. He had to make it out of the evening unscathed, unhurt and still married, those were his objectives. However, the night was still young and now it was the time for games as Hardeep came back up for air 'okay, thanks Gaurav but as I was saying, let's warm things up with a bit of animal fun?'

'With what?' Kully looked at him bemused as did the others. It seemed it was time to confiscate the birthday boy's drinks. Thoughts of being accosted for bestiality offences on his birthday not the majority of the group's idea of a fun evening in.

'Right, if you were an animal what would you be? And to give it gusto you have to name your partner!'

The *'game'* managed to snare the groups attention as they all focussed in on Hardeep. 'Right I will start, and the animal I think would best describe Raj would be... (snake, worm, and fucking whore – oh that's not an animal – these and many other evil thoughts whizzing around in Manjit's head).

Hardeep continued with sickening allure 'she is a butterfly.' The group laughed and roared, the response was terrifyingly loud and dramatic. I mean normally I guess the word butterfly was not that humorous, but with drink clouding their responses; it was right up there with spinning bow ties, clown feet and custard pies in the face.

Hardeep waited for the music of the drunken revellers to die down before elaborating 'and the reason she is a butterfly is because she is colourful and beautiful' The group laughed and Hardeep leant over and kissed his wife on the cheek. Her response was icy cold, her eyes frosted over, but Hardeep did not notice, the drink clouding his judgement in the moment.

The group then took it in turns, Hardeep was a horse because he ate lots of food and had a big head, as described by Raj.

A harsh, but candid revelation, and from the look she cast over to him it appeared not because his schlong was tied to his ankle every day to keep it tamed.

Kully was a cat as she was cuddly and nice to stroke. The bucket was passed around at this stage along with chants of 'you fucking pussy' to the author of that line, a completely inebriated Manjit.

Manjit was described by Kully as a lion, because she had heard that some lions could mate up to 50 times in a single day and that if he had his way then he would overtake that record.

At this juncture Raj chipped in sadistically 'what about now Kully, what's he like? Is he living up to his middle name of Singh (meaning lion)? Kully blushed 'oi cheeky.' She laughed as Manjit stared on in gripped terror as the drink was suitably loosening tongues and making them more and more verbose as the evening wore on. Raj secretly concurred to his pet name of lion, as she knew that she had also gripped his lion's mane many a time in the sheets.

Raj smirked, cackling inwardly 'yeah but you better be careful, you know what these Indian guys are like, if they are not getting some then they will look around for it elsewhere, trust me I know these things'. Hardeep looked at her through sozzled eyes trying to make sense of what she had just said. His face in a concentrated frown, there was some substance to her comments, many a true word said in jest and all that. He did not know what he was looking for, but his recent suspicions of her infidelity were aroused with that comment. The fact that she had said that she knew these things was a close an affirmation of his suspicions then he had needed. Changing the subject deftly and with expert aplomb was Tej.

She then piped up with her animal revelation for her husband Saty shifting Hardeep's focus back on the game and momentarily away from other matters. 'I reckon Saty is a monkey! Tej laughed like a possessed hyena. Her ruse worked as the group turned their heads incredulously looking at her and then at Saty as he sat there arms tucked in between his inner thighs and wolf like frame with shoulders hunched. It was clear from the interaction between them that Tej was the tail that wagged the dog and not the other way around. This was easily decipherable to the others.

Rita looked at Kully and then at Tej, a wry smile appearing on both their faces. They of course knew all about her little secret, and here she was participating in this partner bonding pet name game without a care in the world. Oh the joy of secrets and drinking games, a feisty combination and equalling damning results predicted.

Saty sat there looking on, a silver bullet away from turning into the main lead in the latest werewolf film' A Punjabi werewolf in London' a dead cert winner at the local Southall cinema. Tej chipped in again 'yeah a monkey' Saty slightly confused threw his two pence in 'oh why because I am the king of the swing hey?' He was trying in desperation to salvage some credibility with the group. 'No, no because you are hairier than a woolly mammoth,' she chortled heartily, the sort of laugh that you have every now and then, when you fall back in stitches. Tej held her stomach and looked on full of glee and in between the tears of joy that were rolling down her cheeks.

There were terrified gasps amongst the group. Tej was as pissed as a newt and it seemed spiralling out of control. She was like a runaway train, an untethered bull that had to be tranquillised. Saty glared at her. He was not impressed. He held a tumbler of Jack Daniels with both paws wrapped around it, as you would hold a cup of hot cocoa, sipping from it in similar fashion. The monkey had weird idiosyncrasies, but he didn't care at least his marriage was secure. After all to make it to 4 years in this day and age of opportunity and temptation was a feat in itself he thought as the laughter gradually began to die amongst the revellers. It was he who was having the last laugh he thought smugly to himself.

Rita was then described endearingly as a tigress by her husband. Gaurav then began to justify his choice of animal when Hardeep naughtily interjected 'oh is that because she is good in the sack you sick pervert'. Gaurav grinned with his hands up in the air opened. A gesture telling the group that he didn't know what was meant. Rita played along, assisted tremendously by the alcohol in her system; her expression remained unperturbed by her husband's antics. She would have her day in the sun and within the next few minutes there would be 'khoon kharaba' (bloodshed) that much was certain. All eyes focussed back on Hardeep as the group settled down.

'What now? How about truth or dare?' Gaurav asked as he took hold of a wine bottle tipping it to its side on the carpeted floor.

'Hold on!' a disgruntled voice came back at him. 'What about my turn?' It was Rita. Well of course, it was her turn, how could they have forgotten?

'Yeah I am torn between a couple.' She exclaimed. Gaurav placed the bottle back on the table in nervous anticipation, he winked at Manjit trying to play Jack the lad and Fonzi concomitantly. Like everyone else, he was unsure what was coming despite knowing the cracks that had appeared in the relationship over the last 6 months or so. 'Hmmm, it is out of a snake or a cheetah.' The group sat in stunned and cringing silence. Both words emphasised, enunciated with a gritting of the teeth, a scowl that any evil villain would have been proud.

Gaurav laughed, but after the odd titter, he found himself alone in his chortling as the others looked on at the pair. It was clear that Rita was not joshing, her face as serious as a brain tumour. If she could have sprouted vampire fangs now then it would have added to the sinister intent and malice that her words carried.

The only thing missing was thunder and lightning in the background and some kind of weird '*paagal auntie character*' as there was in the classic Bollywood film '*Phir Wohi Raat*' playing a little number on a piano up in the attic room with her unkempt hair frazzled, frayed and scattered over her head in a shambolic follicular clutter.

Any ambiguity of her description of him was expunged with her next question 'I don't suppose you want to tell the group all about your affairs, your gym bitches who you are screwing hey or do you, save those sorts for the lads?

Gaurav's gulp could be heard in the next town along with the proverbial pin dropping across the road. The sounds of the accompanying violin signalling the final rusty nail in their fledgling relationship could be heard in the background. Raj was simply lapping up the tension, in fact the kuti thrived on it. It was the reason she got out of bed in the morning. Like a couple of twitchy fingered gun slingers Gaurav and Rita sat there eye balling each other. Rita's look rooted deeply in oppression and despair in equal measure, whilst Gaurav was feeling like the Wicker Man walking to his imminent demise and bursting at the seams with fear.

'I am gonna leave now before the biting and scratching starts,' said Manjit to lighten the tension that was building by the second. They ignored his attempt at levity and glared at each other waiting for a reaction.

As the rot continued to set in, the doorbell rang. It was the pizza guy, a life saving and timely intervention. The night was heading towards an otherwise screaming and apocalyptic hell, the warring couple engaged in minimal conversation with one another for the remainder.

The group drank some more wine, rum and other such delights before heartily indulging in the take away pizza.

The delivery man had cut his eyes at the 50p tip that he was feebly offered. His look clearly indicating to a blind man that the next batch of succulent pizzas ordered from their household would have a mouth watering combination of nail clippings, bunion skin, rat fur, bogeys and with a dash of salty 'jis' thrown in for that added '*tang.*'

The evening wore on. The group were one drink away from a coma, and being as drunk as Punjabi Lords.

Hardeep (the brains) pushed the coffee table out of the way with the empty bottles clattering and clunking, some falling to the floor. He then urged the inebriated mob to prepare themselves for a bout of soul baring and soon to be regretted confessions of sin. The group rapidly huddled around into a makeshift circle of sorts, resembling the good old fashioned student days when everyone would find out who was sleeping with who from a few deft twirls of the artful dodger Mr Ron B.

The student games would then naturally progress to the infamous séance. This was where giggling and pissed as fart students would hold hands, sitting cross legged on the floor and trying in vain to wake up the dormant and peaceful spirits of their nanaji or bibiji. The poor cronies having popped their clogs some years ago with sadistic chants of 'come on love, let's have you then. Where you hiding you ole bastards, get your tits out for the lads, this chant was even aimed at grandpa.' This would often be accompanied by strange Twilight Zone music and other such tapping noises.

As the group settled down, Raj, no stranger to controversy leant across to Rita and whispered 'what was all that about before?' her inquisitive approach timed well and catching Rita off guard. 'Oh nothing new, I know he has been shagging around with goria at the gym, the bastard.'

'Really, I never knew.' Raj leaned in even closer, any closer and she would have been sitting in her lap. The queen of gossip just had her front page and headline scoop in her grubby little mitts and this was all without ever having attended a paparazzi course.

'How do you know so?' She stoked the fire a tad more, surely with the drink flowing Rita was not about to pull any punches she had already planned.

'Oh just the odd twenty or so messages that he gets on his phone...the prick thinks I don't know his password.'

Rita's venomous outpouring lighting up Raj's eyes like a Christmas tree.

Just as Raj went in with her next question like the budding journalist she was, Hardeep's deft twirl of the bottle and accompanying cheer set the mood for the real fun that was itching to break out like a bad case of leprosy. The bottle spun impudently snaring its first victim of the evening, – Kully! She immediately aimed her question at Tej. It was perfunctory and as an opening question mildly adequate, but definitely lacking the chutzpah that this game relied heavily upon.

After several bottle spins later, along with several consumed drinks, the mood changed sinisterly with an ambivalent uncertainty. The mugwumps had now been left at the egress as the drinks flowed down the gullets of the intrepid combatants. The bottle neck trickled slowly over around to Saty who sat up eagerly, an evil thought flickering across his mind. He scanned the room assessing suitable bait for his spotlight, and he found one such suitor in the guise of dancing boy. Yes his quarry, sat there with the wide eyed gawk that any would be rabbit would be proud of when staring anxiously into the torch light of the shotgun wielding Elma Fudd type hunter.

'This one is for you Gaurav.' Saty's confidence bolstered with the vat of wine and accompanying whiskies he had consumed as he verbally edged forwards dipping his toe into the lake of curiosity and suitably raising the stakes in an otherwise stupefying game thus far. The sly foxed furby had a loose tongue and fancied trying his luck as he pressed on without remorse or fear for his life. 'So mate, what is your take on affairs then? Do you believe in some cases it is justifiable or not?' His foray into the conversation garnered quizzical looks from the others. He had hacked past the brambles, sheared away the nettles and chopped down the strait jacket of fear that Gaurav had held over him for a long time and cornered his dost like the long whiskered rat he was, by name and nature.

He had not let go of the earlier rumpus between husband and wife and his question was the fuse paper well and truly lit as he sat back paws interlocked on his belly and nestling comfortably on the sofa. Manjit raised his eyebrows whilst looking at Saty's smug expression, nervous that in his drunken state he would be capable of revealing anything, even his sordid affair that he had confessed to him before with the mistress who was sat nearby, and staring at him through the garboil. Although Saty did not know who the mystery girl was, all it took was one unpredictable comment or slip up and the coal would soon begin to kindle in the makeshift furnace of the lounge. Manjit shuffled uneasily in his seat and kept his fingers and toes crossed.

The bait had been set and Gaurav sniffed hard, a way of disguising the shakes or adrenaline skipping around the body when in a fight or flight situation. The sniff worked and his body steadied whilst his mind worked hard to compose an articulate and get out of jail response to his *'friend'*. Gaurav through his drunken stupor had nevertheless grasped the agonising severity of the question. The walls seemingly closing in on him inch by bone busting inch as everyone waited for his monumental belly flop.

'Nice one Saty, and…err…thanks for that you brainless beef head.' Gaurav was not impressed but now all eyes fell on him. His thoughts momentarily thinking of how a melee weapon would sort the situation out, gunning them all down like lemmings as he made his great escape.

His mental turmoil was short lived as he found himself speaking, his lips moving, extemporising without his official command, no doubt spurred on by uncle Ron and his staunch comrades.

'Yeah I think affairs are okay.' His claims asserting clearly that guys have a predilection for infidelity. The shaking of the heads from Manjit and Hardeep simultaneously were sure fire signs that they knew that Gaurav, when drunk was the worlds most loquacious soap box performer, and here he had a stage, a captive audience and not to mention a meaty subject; the world was his oyster. The cut and thrust of the evening had now reached its painful climax and it had all the makings of a miserable ending for all concerned. Everyone looked on in silent consternation.

'Well if you are asking me if I think it is right or if it is okay to go behind your partners back then I think if you have got problems in your relationship then yeah why not. It is one way to straighten out the hairpins in your marriage isn't it?'

Gaurav scanned the room for reactions to his opinions on the subject.

'What are we some kind of pining Labradors who wait for their wives to throw a ball up in the air so we can fetch it, sod that shit, If things are wrong in the marriage go get some dog.'

He continued to hold court in loquacious fashion, 'yeah what are you supposed to do if you have got problems and your partner refused to put out, ask yourself that?'

It was clear to all and sundry that his vehement outpouring was being directed squarely at Rita's door, this was without question despite his generic and surreptitious smokescreen.

His worm ridden words, slithering there way out of his cake hole, and not impressing the flogging mob who fiendishly sat there staring at him slowly tossing their rotten tomatoes up and down in their hands.

He was far from finished. Here he was a raconteur, a maestro of the spoken word in his finest moment. His Oscar winning performance being played out to all of them. He rambled on 'people have needs and at the end of the day it is only a physical release isn't it. The great emperors of the past, in fact all throughout history it is written everywhere that all these soldiers, tribes, kings and emperors would bang a fresh girl every night. It was accepted and there was none of the brainwashing rubbish that we are all drip fed about only having one girl or guy. You know what I mean.' There were eyebrows raising all around the room and Rita couldn't resist. The bait was sitting there on the hook with two fingers and its tongue sticking out, goading her into entering the fray. It was not the kind of love potion envisaged that the game had promised to produce.

The seconds ticked by as his words sunk in, the damning moment churning painfully forward. Suddenly the silence was shattered emphatically 'that's such bullshit.' There were gasps all over, with everyone momentarily snapping out of their drunken stupors. 'Nonsensical rubbish. So, you condone people having affairs? That says a lot about you.' Rita snapped at him. Her arms folded and with unbending features.

'Oh here she goes, the mouth, yeah the mouth on a stick is off, brace yourself folks, blah blah blah.' Gaurav moved his right hand in front of his face as he moved his fingers and thumb up and down towards each other mimicking someone who is talking incessantly, a chatterbox or nagging aficionado. 'I call her the nagging lobster.' He pointed his eyes towards his puppet hand intimating that her mouth was like that of a lobsters claw hand opening and snapping shut.

This teasing and flapping of the red cloth was only exacerbating the situation as Rita lunged for him. She was quickly held back by Tej and Kully and restrained back on the sofa. His earthquake like response belittling his wife and uprooting any dignity she had. He may as well have got back on the table with his todger out and pissed all over her; at least then, his words would have been backed up his actions.

Raj looked on excitedly, almost climaxing over the domestic being played out sublimely before her very eyes. The pair continued to bicker and attack one another with low swiping blows ensuring they were ahead in the point scoring league table. 'Oi it is my birthday guys. Come on chill out for a flipping second will you.' He managed to diffuse the tension as Gaurav stood up and walked out of the room to visit the boys room.

Raj then for some reason decided to ramp the stakes up and added to the masala mix 'all guys are weak. All you have to do is engage the little brain and they will follow you around like love sick puppies complete with wet noses and drooping eyes.' They all listened with Manjit squirming uncomfortably in his seat, he knew what was coming and there was no way of stopping the inevitable now. He just prayed she dealt the blow to him like a trained soldier. A short, sharp and decisive blow to end the misery. He had never felt more suicidal as he did now, the torment and burgeoning guilt of the mess his life was becoming was over whelming. Worst of all he knew that his impending doom loomed by virtue of her forthcoming disembowelling words.

She ranted on 'I find it fascinating looking at their desperate, grasping looks plastered across their faces when the mere hint of sex is on the cards, watch them speak in monosyllables in between fiddling with their crotches at the very thought of getting some. It is all in the math.' She spoke like the true nymphomaniac that she was revered as, her specialist mastermind subject *'nookie.'*

'Yeah but why is that guys always blame someone else or come out with a lame excuse when they have an affair. All the usual one's come out. It is the wife she doesn't give it to me. Oh I am a sex addict, I just wanted to try someone different.' Rita preached to the group.

The drink, the tensions, and the time in the evening had made the conversation skittish and discursive as they sloped from subject to subject in rapid succession.

'Hey Kully, how is your brother Joe these days? Is he still a nutter as I remember him? Tej asked her friend. Kully's brother's reputation preceding him. His hair trigger temper the cause of all his skirmishes in the past. 'Yeah he is okay, I spoke to him yesterday, he says hello to you guys.'

Whilst that conversation was going on Gaurav who had now returned to the group turned to Manjit 'dude, that was close.' Manjit put his arm around him and squeezed him as a term of affection, he had always liked Gaurav. He was the kind of guy who always spoke his mind and didn't care what anything thought about him. He was a live and die by the sword kind of guy.

'Hey despite all that shit before, I still want to get my missus pregnant, if she will ever sleep with me again. Then she will have to stay cos she will have a kid and baggage, ha ha.' Gaurav bragged to Manjit with the stench of booze engulfing his friend.

Gaurav rambled on 'it is much harder for an Asian girl to walk away when she has the baggage of kids, as much as every fibre in her body will tell her to walk; she will find that small crumb of compassion for the kids sake, to stay and make a go of things and trust me I know that. They will always stay for the sake of the kids.' He flexed two fingers on each hand to represent inverted comma's to emphasise his statement.

Gaurav was merely trying in vain to carry out the all time classic manoeuvre and in some cases impeccably actioned by some very insecure and often *'friggin fugly'* guys who happened to land themselves a half decent looker of a wife. His sentiments were laughed off by Manjit as he tuned to see if Raj had made anymore revelations in her speaker's corner across the room. Gaurav meanwhile drank another glass of wine, without remorse.

The evening drew to a close and the couples all began to head off home. Manjit was speaking to Hardeep in the kitchen; he wanted to know if Raj had mentioned anything to him or if he was aware that she was HIV positive. 'How are things between you and your missus bro?' Manjit asked tentatively.

'Not great mate to be honest. I am a bit suspicious.' Hardeep looked over Manjit's shoulder to make sure there was no other frequency tuned in on their conversation. 'I think she might be seeing someone, I have thought this for a while.'

'What, how do you know that?' Manjit's reaction almost too revealing in the circumstances, but luckily not picked up by his normally shrewd brother. 'Well we have been having problems for a while, we sleep in separate rooms and all that. We might even break up.' His voice remained a matter of fact.

'Tell me truthfully, are you checking some next girl out?' Manjit whispered. Hardeep's face beamed into a smile, his pantomimes (facial non verbal signals) sending a clear message to his brother. He went on to elaborate when without cue Rita popped her head through the kitchen door 'okay guys I am off.'

'What about Gaurav?' Manjit asked.

'Tell him the taxi is outside, he has got 2 minutes.' Her no nonsense approach laying it down crisp and curt.

'See you tomorrow Kully, Raj for a coffee. You sure you can't make it?' She asked Tej as they were all putting their coats on in the hallway. 'No, no I have, err, got an appointment tomorrow morning, but...erm...I will see you tomorrow evening okay.' Rita shifted her eyes side-ward's looking at Kully who reciprocated the shifty look and attempted to stifle her laugh.

Within the next 10 minutes and at 1am the three taxi's had arrived and whisked them all off to their respective homes. The evening had left many burning questions unanswered, many problems unresolved and explosive secrets waiting in the shadows ready to shatter someone's life...and as they say, when you lie once, then you have to keep covering that lie until you get away with it or you slip up...

Chapter 14

'Latte' it go

The next morning Rita, Kully and Raj all met up for a coffee and some shopping in the Treaty Centre, with the subject of the previous evening's tumultuous events being the main topic of discussion. Last night was not the ideal time to chat away freely without the others eaves dropping on their conversations, and there was the delicate investigation into their other friend's infidelity to be thrashed and bottomed out.

'Well girls, what the hell happened last night?' Raj laughed aiming her question indirectly towards Rita and her dirty washing moment with Gaurav. They all laughed. 'Oh you don't want to know.' Rita picked up the hint and rebuffed her interrogative probing, maybe she did not feel like discussing her love life now that she was sober and in the cold light of the day.

'Oh but we do want to know.' Raj retorted swiftly keeping her beady eyes fixed on Rita over the rim of her cup of latte.

Like a dog with a stick, she would not let it go and her tenacity paid dividends as Rita sung like a canary. 'Where do I start, he has been sleeping around and rubbing my nose in it. He thinks he is untouchable or something and that I will stick around while he does my beesti.' The existence of her husband's parallel world making her a prey to anxiety. 'I am better than that and I deserve better. I am no doormat.' Her lucid response choked with cliché. The air of exuberance surrounding Raj at this moment was almost palpable as she listened intently.

Kully leant over and hugged her friend 'don't worry we are here for you if you need to talk.'

Her heartfelt reassurance edifying Rita and helping her rationalise the pain she was having to endure. Meanwhile Raj smirked in her cup of latte, a window of opportunity had presented itself and the cogs turned malevolently within her head.

'Anyway can we change the subject, my head is still pounding from last night and I will end up getting depressed or hitting the bottle, one or the other, you know hair of the kuta and all that.' The girls laughed. She was referring to the old wives tale that by drinking some more booze in the morning after a heavy alcoholic binge was said to settle the bodies system and help cure a hangover. This was derived from the belief that by placing a dog's hair over the bite would assist in helping the wound to heal quicker and act as an antidote.

'Okay what the hell is going on with Tej hey?' Kully broached the burning question on all their minds and sat forward eager to delve into her friends extra marital interests, as they all were. 'Well come on can you blame her?' The voice of moral rectitude spoke, and the natural authority on the subject of such trysts, Raj. She justified her comment 'have you seen the guy? I mean I have seen better looking beasts in captivity at Battersea dogs home, come on.' Her scathing rebuke an obvious sleight regarding his hirsute and canine like fur smattered around his frame.

'I was speaking to Tej a few months ago and we got into our husbands mannerisms and habits. Do you know that he is a slob; he is addicted to porn, he is obviously hairy.' Kully interjected in his defence 'oh come on you are just focussing in on his bad points. The guy is okay, poor thing.

Raj was just warming up as she went in again. 'Oh yeah he cuts nails everywhere; picks his nose in front of the TV; has got really cheesy feet which he sits there wagging all day; and above all he has got breath that could strip paint.' Raj leaned back in her chair and cackled away her eyes filling with water from the sheer joy of her indefensible onslaught. Her witch like cackling brought uneasy looks from shoppers who were walking past their al fresco coffee table on the first floor of the centre.

'She is just saying that cos she wants to have him.' Kully mocked her friend as her cackling slowly died down. Raj not one to be belittled easily, and keen to get the last word, snapped back sharply. 'Put it this way I would rather drive nails through my eyes or go on a dinner date with Hannibal Lecter than sleep with him. No offence but the guy is deathly boring and not at all sexy!'

'It has to be a marriage of convenience and yeah I agree she is an ideal candidate for an affair especially after what I saw the other day.' Rita added.

'What happened the other day?' Raj rested her hands on the table to illicit more gossip from her and diverting her attention away from her childish bickering with Kully for a moment.

Rita then regaled her with the sighting of Tej and her mystery man at her house when Saty was off the scene. She emphasised that she had never seen Tej acting so furtively and awkward as she had seen when she was searching the street in case anyone had seen her fancy man. 'No way.' Raj almost fell off her chair in sheer delight as another scoop and bombshell was dropped for her delectation.

'Yeah but you can clearly see that Saty is very loyal…despite the fact that he is a bloke.' Kully's assessment was accurate.

'Nah I can't see it from her point of view. I mean she scrubs up okay, but him, seriously.'

Raj was remorseless in her summing up. She continued with devious spitefulness 'they had an arranged marriage. You know the sort, when you go on the say so of your parents because it will make them happy. But, mum, dad no disrespect, but I am the one who has to shag the guy and live with him all my life. Thanks but no thanks. If you like him that much then you marry him.' Raj's disrespectful tone cutting and downright evil and not going down too well with Kully.

It appeared to her that Raj was almost condoning the fact that Tej was seeing someone behind her husbands back. Only a vindictive and warped person would want such a pervading atmosphere of duplicity and unhappiness for her close friends. At that single moment Kully had developed an underbelly of resentment and disgust in her friends perceived behaviour, just like she had on many occasions as they grew up together on the gritty streets *'of the big H.'*

'Then again, I still think he is a good bloke and if she is cheating on him, well then I am going to say something.' Kully purposefully slipped her viewpoint into the flow of the conversation knowing full well that it was contradictory to that of Raj and secondly because she genuinely cared for Saty. He had never done her any harm and her loyalty to a friend was endearing.

Raj picked the baton up and ran with it 'oh yeah he is as endearing as a cup of cold and frothy piss. I mean come on he is a slob, no ifs or buts, a knuckle scraping Neanderthal who burps, farts and slithers through life, lovely.'

Rita jumped in at this moment. She too had something useful to add 'so let me get this straight, he wags his feet, picks his nose, smells like a dead skunk, and slobs in front of the box all day. Great at least you know he is a sure bet and god damn wouldn't cheat on you.' They all laughed unsure whether she was actually being serious or if she was poking fun.

'He is a catch.' Raj mocked. 'Oh and I have heard you lot say that they are the perfect couple...seriously don't give me that rubbish, when something is too good to be true, it usually means it normally is too good to be true.' Her voice turned serious and sinister 'and now she is getting her kicks somewhere else, hmmm.'

No-one spoke as they sat there looking around the Treaty Centre in contemplative thought.

'Anyway what has it got to do with me? Raj announced. 'If she is cheating then I say it is up to her. Personally, he doesn't sizzle my sausages, I know life can be cruel and the good guys get wasted first and all that, but my advice is he would do well to grow a pair and then maybe she wouldn't stray.'

Raj then stood up abruptly and put her coat on. 'Look I will see you both tonight...I have to go.' Her behaviour was bizarre and with that she walked away blending into the crowd of shoppers before the girls could react. The HIV letter was still hanging over her head, along with her hankering to be with Manjit both palpable reasons for her irrational deportment.

Kully and Rita finished up and went on to do a spot of shopping hotly discussing what had just occurred and trying to make sense of it. The shelter and comfort of all their relationships were slowly being burnt to a crisp in the smouldering flames of forbidden extra marital lust and chicanery. The evening ahead promised to be terrifyingly compelling and calamitous for every one of them. There was simply no escape as the executioner of veracity beckoned them...

—ᴍ—

Feisty girls

That evening the boys had decided to hook up and hit the local bars like the flamboyant socialites they were with their usual uncontrollable verve, whilst the girls a chance to kick back and chill within the comfort of Tej's living room.

This day had been arranged a few weeks ago and it was a chance for everyone to let their hair down and blow the cobwebs out of the system in riveting company, all the girls on one side and all the testosterone lads on the other side of the fence, each with their own agenda's. Hardeep's birthday the day before had been a mere warm up.

The rendezvous point was planned at Tej and Saty's house at 7pm and by around 7.45pm all four couples were in fine fettle, knocking back desi shots and quality controlling all manner of feisty cocktails. The name of the game tonight was to get plastered with all recipients charged up for the ensuing battle ahead. The living room was majestically resplendent with the mantelpiece adorned with artefacts and souvenirs from their recent trip to Turkey, the remainder of the room furnished lavishly with accoutrements and chattels of the highest calibre.

At 8pm, the taxi bibbed the horn from outside the house and the lads were heading for the egress like a pack of drink thirsty mutts. They walked out into the cool evening breeze, the air licking them and fuelling the alcohol in their system almost like the effect of a back draft in a blazing fire. Within a few seconds the front door slammed shut with the boys shuttling down the road in the taxi – destination *'Drink Town.'*

The girls immediately swung into the groove with determined fervency being careful not to waste a precious second of drinking. The drinks were consumed in disturbingly copious amounts, with the *desi gals* proving their worth in the drinking stakes and more than a match for their spouses. The rigours of work were slowly melting away from their battered and bruised souls with an air of reverential relaxation like a soothing blanket around their weary shoulders.

The conversation switched deftly from subject to subject with the drink making the topics juicier by the second. The girls lounging around the room sat on the black leather three seat and two seat sofas, shoes off and in a relaxed and quintessentially refreshed mood. The TV in the background drowned out by their incessant and feverish chatter.

'Come on let's talk about our other halves then.' Raj said stoking the fire with her pitchfork, the red horns slowly appearing from her head. 'What's Saty like? You know generally?' her attention focussed primarily on Tej.

'Oh he is well okay.' Tej purred trying not to give too much away with her carefully pitched response, her feeble bid to hoodwink the group immediately detected by an alert Rita who knew only too well about her day time sexual release a few days earlier.

Rita glared at Tej pondering her motivation for cheating, her mind a repository of knowledge as the chill of duplicity persistently hummed around them. Her pondering suddenly stopped when she remembered that she was after all married to Tarzans sidekick *'Cheetah.'*

The conversation mood had now changed significantly with the log that Raj had sneakily thrown onto the furnace, and with the drink flowing, the questions became more and more penetrative. A dark cloud had begun to descend above them but they had not realised yet.

During the conversation, Kully chipped in with her take on her husband. 'Manj is awesome in every way, and I know he totally loves me, he is the Taj Mahal of husbands, he truly is.' She appeared to blush and her effervescent smile beamed across her face.

'They say that a marriage that is not built on wild and passionate sex is doomed from the outset, because in those tough times that is what you will fall back on,' she laughed. 'Although we have been taking it a bit easy in that department recently I know that our love is still there and that is the main thing isn't it?'

The words gushing out of her mouth as she scanned the room for the group's reaction. Raj returned her friends outpouring of undying love and worshipping with contempt and self satisfaction as the thoughts of her very own clandestine moments with the same *'Taj Mahal husband'* continued to whirr in her mind with heinous pleasure in this game of one up man ship.

'Yeah, so what are you saying, is that he would never look at another girl, or say cheat on you?' The cat was now pawing at the mouse, the snake charmer captivating the snake with his music, the hunter (alright, alright we get the picture).

Raj now had her in the vice and was rotating the handle teasingly by the second and revelling in the moment of opacity.

'Yeah I don't have to think about it, I know he would never do that. When you have the kind of relationship we have then you know that (she laughed to herself) is just a silly remark to make, so...'

'Oh so you know where he is 24/7 do you, well do you? Don't forget he is a guy, and that makes him dangerous (an involuntary wry smirk appeared on her face which she done well to stifle) and I should know.' She mumbled before lifting her glass to her heavily coated red lipstick.

'What was that?' Kully asked sitting up on the sofa where she was sitting opposite Raj. The febrile atmosphere had now been cranked up, she dimmed the volume of the TV down a few notches because she was intent on catching the sly remark that Raj had made in her concluding statement. Raj said nothing but just looked, the bunny boiling persona soothingly suppressed for the time being.

Kully repeated herself 'what did you say about you knowing?' Her voice and tone punctuated with curiosity, with a hint of angst.

'Oh shut up! What do you know about what goes on in your perfect little world, get out there and smell the reality...' Raj responded curtly and with clinching proof that there was an underlying reason for her remarks.

Kully controlled her response, looking at Rita and Tej incredulous to Raj's sniping and jaundiced remarks.

'Anyway if I wanted to I could have him easy...and who knows maybe I already have...' Raj was self satisfied that she had just tarnished the sanctity of her friend's marriage.

Kully looked on stunned, she had just been served up a teaspoon of bitchery and metaphorically began lacing up her boxing gloves, seconds away from putting in her mouth guard from the other side of the room.

Kully had heard enough, and her plain Jane persona when hurtling out of the window without further ado as Raj's goading had pierced a wound so deep and unforgivable that her reaction came as no surprise for the gaggle of girls gathered in the room this evening. The atmosphere had turned nasty as the heat and hustle of the get together brimmed menacingly towards a show down of sorts.

'Look here you kunjari. If you had any thought about anyone but yourself you would realise the damage and hurt you have caused with your stupid and irresponsible words and teasing.'

Her venomous outpouring was striking a chord with Raj, who now began to lift her body off the sofa. Tej and Rita meanwhile looked on hoping and praying that the pair of them would back down before they became embroiled in a dissention.

She stared at Kully, her nostrils flaring and her spurs jangling in preparedness for the inevitable duel that was imminent. Kully slowly stood up in the middle of the room, her hands on her hips, her body swaying slightly from the copious amounts of alcohol that she had perilously consumed throughout the course of the evening, a lethal concoction of Jack Daniels, Baileys and a couple of glasses of wine adding to the swirling tempestuousness.

She inched forward as Raj who began fiddling with her neck chain looked up at her from her seated and vulnerable position, her green eyes staring back like mini saucers but without a trace of residual guilt anywhere to be seen.

'I mean who the hell do you think you are? You think it is funny to talk about stealing someone else's husband? Go and get a life...you haramzadi, kunjari, slapper...' Kullys voice a state of excited delirium as she waved her arms around like a Thunderbird puppet.

'Oh shut up, kuti, kaminee...miss goody two shoes' Raj shouted back sensing her disquiet and having heard enough lecturing for one evening.

She stood up and moved closer to Kully standing face to face with her nemesis, toe to toe and handbag to handbag.

'You open your legs for anyone you filthy tart, you are the gundiest harami I know' Kully was swift with her retort, the drink transforming her dramatically.

'Yeah, well at least I am not deluded by thinking my husband is a saint you daft, ditsy bitch. Wake up and smell the fact that I have loved having him behind your back.'

The jaundiced words quickly filled Kully's heart with a sea of pure disgust, a stinging burn of resentment.

Raj had only just started her verbal diatribe and slurred on 'yeah it was good...especially when he whispers how much he loves doing it with me, ha.' An aura of self satisfaction gripping her tone as the words shuttled out into the room adding a murderous haze around the girls.

Raj's churlish words shattering the very foundations and sanctum of Kully's life and marriage.

'You should know how to satisfy your man or if not you better sign those divorce papers quickly and have done with it, cos he don't love you, it's me he wants to be with, ask him if you don't believe me.'

How and why would she be so vindictive to say such hurtful things about her husband? Kully shook her head and looked around at Tej and Rita, hoping and pleading for this to be some kind of sick joke.

Her friends now stood around the pair of them, concerned, devastated, but equally helpless as the reality of the situation was driven home to Kully like the proverbial stake through the heart as the perpetrator, smug, cocky and wallowing in her anguished pain was stood teasingly before her.

The bait had been set and without a skip of the heartbeat Kully lunged forward, she could take no more, the ferocity and bile of Raj's words had cut into her, charging her anger up. Kully violently grabbed Raj by her hair with both of her hands and tugged her forward with great ferocity catching her cheating friend totally by surprise. Raj may have been one step ahead in deceiving those around her by sneaking around behind Kully's back but she had not calculated the unrelenting fury that Kully was in the throes of unleashing now that the truth lay bare this evening.

Like a tag team of wrestling referees, Rita and Tej tried in vain to separate them but their efforts were proving futile. Raj and Kully remained locked together like a couple of snorting bulls in the middle of the room, the only thing missing was the mud.

In the violent rumpus that was in mid flow both hapless friends – Tej and Rita were tossed like capers, shrugged off and swatted backwards by the rapid and twisting movements form the sparring warriors on centre stage. Raj naturally tried to pull back and away from the rampaging and marauding attack from Kully. She wrestled in vain lifting her arms up and hanging onto Kully's hair as a natural defence mechanism.

The pair of them wrestled 'kutee, harami, you fucking whore, how dare you try to wreck my marriage…' Kully screamed as she managed to trip Raj up onto the sofa in a move that would have had any WWE wrestler saluting her prowess and guile. They both landed with a sickening crunch, Kully on top of Raj.

Like a cartoon character Kully's fists suddenly ballooned into large anvils, twice the size and she began pounding down on her hapless and equally soused amigo with merciless fury whilst Raj tried in vain to stem the flow by holding on to her hair like a rodeo - CRUNCH, SMASH, WALLOP, THUD.

As they continued to fight, Raj suddenly let go of her hair, realising with great fighting instinct that her face was unprotected from the freefall of strikes landing like bombs. Kully continued to rain a succession of thudding blows down on her head as Raj desperately covered her pretty face with her arms whilst wriggling around for all her worth expertly evading the majority of blows with aplomb, her fistfuls of pure hatred.

Tej had seen enough and using her body launched herself in-between the pair of them in true Bollywood fashion placing herself in harms way. She was a martyr, without a care for her own safety as she wedged herself in the middle of them deflecting Kully's fists, slaps and scratches that were reigning down rapidly not to mention alcohol stained saliva dripping from Kully's mouth, like a St Bernard dog and down onto her hair.

She lay on top of the cowering Raj employing this tactic out of necessity to dissolve the fight, and essentially before eyeballs rolled across the living room or limbs were ripped off and dangled in the air as trophies.

In the meantime, Rita took a hold of Kully's shoulders and using all her might managed to wrench her friend off her prey falling back with her onto the floor smashing the coffee table against the television. Kully however was undeterred and had tasted blood, she wriggled to break free form Rita who was laying beneath her flattened and nursing bruised ribs in the fall.

She regained her footing and with gritted teeth moved forward again, her hair dishevelled, clothes tattered, torn, and hobbling with one shoe on with the other shoe having been flung across the room by the window in the melee. Tej stood up and seizing the momentary lapse in the rumpus managed to quickly usher Raj out of the room using her body as a shield and obscuring the flailing arms and pointing finger of Kully as she tried in vain to finish off the job.

Raj stood by the door of the living room and went to walk out but stopped. Tej looked nervously over her shoulder whilst trying to contain Kully by pushing her back every time she tried to lunge past. Rita similarly stepped in front of Kully and next to Tej to form an impenetrable dam suitably containing the snarling beast in the form of Kully who was pacing up and down trying to get at her meal that was stood at the door putting her red heeled shoes back on, but in a somewhat leisurely fashion.

'Look just get out of here, you are both drunk and it will kick off again…just go.' The desperation in Tej's voice was tangible.

The mascara on Kully's face started to run as the tears streamed down her face, a fiery combination of the prospect of her marriage collapsing and the thoughts of her 'friend' being the wielder of the executioners axe was all too consuming for her to comprehend. The adrenal dump had now kicked in and had Kully plunging back forceless and onto her weakened haunches.

The tears rolled unceremoniously and without a shred of remorse, trickling and snaking their way around her lips and chin. She resembled an ancient tribal warrior with the black streaks painted on her cheeks, the red marks on her neck beginning to sting and her hair the after effects of placing your finger into an electric socket.

Tej's living room looked like it had been hit by a grenade with broken wine glasses strewn about, drink spillages everywhere, a television that had toppled over, the coffee table merely standing upright with three legs, the fourth leg snapped in two and dangling by a couple of wooden fibres.

Overall, it was enough to give Tej a heart attack being the domestic goddess that she was. Selfishly her thoughts were preoccupied with the disaster movie her living room was than the actual beef between her hell bent and demented friends feud with one another.

Raj stood across from them preening herself in the hallway mirror, her main concerns for her face as she had eaten a swingeing amount of blows. She had miraculously managed to avoid been marked, save for a few blotchy patches of red skin on her neck and arms. 'I am going now, but hey don't worry I am sure he doesn't think about me too much when he is doing it with you. She snarled teasingly. 'Then again, maybe he does, because he told me that is exactly what happens...he

closes his eyes and imagines that it is me he is screwing.'
Her actions and face that of a maggot.

Raj had the last word; she swivelled on the spot and
walked out of the room. The front door was heard slamming shut and the sound of her walking down the drive
slowly tapering out. The home breaker had left the
saloon and for all intent and purposes had rubbed
Kully's nose in the tutti and that was unforgivable.
Kully's self confidence had eroded. The pungent aroma
of failure stamped on her forehead as she continued
crying grievously. She was left in her own squalor, her
reputation and standing now in tatters and crumbling
into a pile of dirt on the floor, her eyes moist and burning with grief. Where would she go from here?

CHAPTER 16

—⁓—

Plethora of mahi's

During the fireworks that were exploding at the girls get together, the boys had started equally well with the drink flowing soothingly. The taxi had dropped them all off at 'The Tabla Tavern' a local haunt for the trendy crowd, a wall to wall display of sartorial elegance guaranteed. The lads were impeccably suited and booted in their ensemble with Gaurav standing out head and shoulders above the rest of the rabble with the white collars of his shirt flicked up, his shirt covered by his black Armani sweater. His black jeans tightly cut and caressing his sculptured thighs, the thighs that had melted the eyes and hearts of many impressionable senorita's over the years. His appearance capped off with his snazzy black Italian shoes. He was off the sizzle Richter Scale and he knew it as they cruised up to the entrance of Tabla Tavern.

'Come on let's get hammered tonight.' Gaurav egged on the others as they entered. There were a good mixture of people strewn throughout the Tavern and the night promised to be action packed, in many ways.

They stood by the bar making small talk. Gaurav turned to Saty 'get the pints in sunshine.' Saty responded by taking out his wallet, the moths fluttering around them and almost taking out their eyes.

Manjit whispered to Gaurav 'geezer, go easy on him tonight, okay.' Manjit knew full well that Gaurav had a memory like an elephant and would be remembering the awkward question that Saty posed for him last night which nigh on resulted in a blood bath and from his hostility it appeared that he was not about to forgive and forget. 'Nah don't worry, the only reason I am saying that is because he is a bit conclusively retentive if you catch my drift.' Manjit looked confused 'he is what?'

'A tight wad that's what.' Gaurav's answer added clarity to Manjit's ambiguity.

'Anyway tonight I am the pantheon of Greek Gods.' Gaurav chirped.

Meanwhile Hardeep managed to secure a table by the window. He stood by it guarding it like a sentry, warning off any potential squatters with an evil glare seen more commonly in horror films by a sadistic and deranged serial killer. It worked, and there remained a sterile zone around him for the few minutes it took the others to join him with their beers.

Manjit had noticed that his brother had already looked out of the window several times as they settled down, as though expecting something to happen, he found this strange.

The guys all sat in their chairs and toasted each other with their pints clinking in the middle whilst simultaneously shouting *'chitters up'* the Punjabi version of *'salud'* as said by the Italians. The Punjabi version basically meaning *'bottoms up.'*

The guys drank away and kept their eyes fixed around the boozer, searching for and commenting on every piece of female arse that walked past, married, single, co-habiting, gay – it did not matter one drop, as every red blooded male in the establishment were doing just that, after all it was the main reason they wanted to go out. As someone had once said, that life without sex is the sign that you are dead – from within!

The conversation deepened as the drink flowed in their systems, as did the boisterous behaviour, the drinking games and mindless chatting up of scattered females lounging around different areas of the bar. They all laughed through the excited and bubbly atmosphere. The bar continued to liven up with the throng of revellers getting into the party spirit.

'Oi kuta, how is your sex life then?' Gaurav asked the shrinking violet Saty as he supped on his beer quietly in the corner.

Saty looked across at Gaurav in trepidation. It was clear that he was already becoming brash and swaggering despite there being plenty of mileage left in the evening. He thought best that he responded 'yeah it is okay, apart from the odd headache here and there, ha ha.'

The group all laughed. Gaurav came back at him straight away, 'oi don't forget inside every woman is a whore waiting to be discovered. So next time she does that shit with you about having a headache, yeah, stick an aspirin on the tip of your piece and say now suck on that and everyone is a winner.' His words of wisdom enunciated with such equanimity.

Gaurav laughed hard, so much so that it triggered off a coughing and spluttering fit that ended with him being patted on the back several times by Hardeep. He sat back down momentarily as Saty looked on in quiet disdain at his worsening condition. The guy was a walking conun-drum, a human sudoku puzzle waiting to be solved. There was no rhyme or reasoning to his outlandish laddish behaviour, but he could sense that things were about to go from bad, to worse.

'Oi remember that time when Saty passed out after we went out boozing and we got some hair remover spray and put a Nike tick on his back. That was well funny.' Gaurav shared his joke with half of the patrons in the bar with his loud booming voice echoing over the normal pitched conversations that were going. Saty cringed in his seat and at this point had wished he had stayed at home, he was sure the situation was about to exacerbate sooner rather than later such was Gaurav's pestiferous actions that evening. Across the bar someone waited patiently, watching and sizing them up. The group were being studied, every action, every joke and every movement noted down mentally. The stranger remained hidden in the shadows of the bar.

'Better still remember that girl that Hardeep pulled year's ago.' Manjit laughed as he sipped from his pint. Hardeep sat a little more uneasy in his seat. 'Yeah you know the gargoyle. I mean her beauty was so intoxi-cating, what was her name?' The guys searched hard racking their frame's of reference when suddenly they erupted with a chorus of 'yeah we remember.'

'I mean come on man, you into mutants or some-thing. I could just imagine waking up next to her every morning as she fumbles around to stick her contact lenses into her three eyes.' Hardeep laughed and imme-diately looked out through the window, a vacuous look in his eyes. The guys fell about laughing. The banter and joviality was exchanged by all of them with the atmosphere continually convivial.

No sooner had the commotion died down when Gaurav stood up and knocked back a slug of Bacardi and coke before announcing that he would try to chat up the most hideous creature in the bar for a wind up. He started the bidding at £10 each if he could bring the nearest monster over and ask her out in front of the baying mob. Manjit and Hardeep slammed their £10 on the table, as did Saty after initial persuasion from the others.

The bounty remained firmly in place and wedged underneath a half empty pint of beer in the centre of the table as Gaurav's eyes, like a submarine captain scoured the room with deadly menace. He looked hard and thoroughly when suddenly – ding, dong, there she was the object of his disaffection, standing there 20 feet away and with the National Lottery finger pointing down above her head, all 18 stone of her, the goddess of cream pies and corpulent pie scoffing larder monster. 'There she is.' He pointed to her whilst smiling wryly. 'The girl with the wiry mop on her head,' he indicated. All eyes suddenly locked their sights on the subject of Gaurav's wind up standing blissfully unaware several feet away.

He winked at the guys as he edged himself out around the table and headed over to her. The damsel in distress was embroiled in conversation with another girl and completely unaware of the tsunami honing in on her.

At that moment, she coincidentally turned and was about to head to the ladies room when she stopped in her tracks. There stood a mere gnat's pubic hair away from her, was the suave and handsomely turned out Gaurav. He smiled ala Shah Rukh Khan and immediately buckled her knees; this was more from the shift of weight from her gut as she had turned too quickly. Gaurav sized her up and quickly engaged in nonsensical conversation with her lathering her up with his smooth chat up lines. His verbal dexterity in any given situation, always being one of his fortes.

This went on for a few moments as the remaining boys looked on in eager and sadistic anticipation. Suddenly Gaurav began to walk back towards them triumphantly as the booby prize trailed behind him like an autobot. He had almost succeeded and the money pot teasingly beckoned him. The patrons in the bar were parting fan like as they walked through such was her hulking presence, at one stage it was almost like a disaster movie with people screaming and running around the pub with both arms held aloft and seeking to escape as the end of level heaving monster rampaged and terrorised the villagers.

Finally, they had made it to the table without any army helicopters being deployed and circling the beast from above in a bid to gun her down.

'Guys this is the scrumptious Nita.' Gaurav stretched his arm out as he welcomed his guest to the group. There was a spice to his voice, a cold arrogance. He was at his most voluble and witty when he had drink cascading through his system and the group knew this.

Saty could be seen shaking his head in utter dismay. He knew Gaurav too well and feared what was about to unfold. 'She has agreed to go out with me next week.' He muttered cruelly. Nita nodded enthusiastically, her naivety, and vulnerability exposed in the most deplorable fashion as Gaurav wallowed in her public demise. It was at this point that he scooped up the winnings in his hand

and cheered 'yyyyesssss!' whilst lifting his arm in the air as though he had just scored a goal. Vulgar and distasteful were his bywords and the looks of disapproval were reverberating around him much to his blissful ignorance.

Nita at 23 years old was young and impressionable and suddenly woke up and smelt the chaa. If she was in any doubt about the mystery stranger's intentions then this was eradicated when Gaurav in a sudden paroxysm of laughter reached up and for some bizarre reason ran his hand deep into the shock of black hair scrunched up over her skull. He rummaged for a few seconds before pulling it out slowly as though examining a rare disease. 'AAAGGHHH!' He yelled as the gooey oil extracted from within stuck to his hand like leprosy. Droplets of a secret Asian oil seeped through his fingers. The pungent waft immediately struck the group as everyone instinctively held their noses in discomfort.

Gaurav quickly leaned over and wiped his hand against the back of the padded comfort chair that lay situated behind him. The guys lurched back in horror and Nita ran off crying. His cruel and heartless actions had ruined her night as she fled from the scene of the crime, the saloon doors flapping wildly behind her as she galloped into the red sequinned wash of the evening sky never to be seen again that evening. Her friend looked disgusted and similarly walked out of the door wounded vicariously for her friend's humiliation. Gaurav shrugged her look off and continued to examine his hands for signs of long term damage such was his angst at discovering half of the worlds oil reserves nestled secretively in her bonce.

All throughout this incident Manjit had noticed that Hardeep was becoming increasingly fidgety and kept looking out of the bar window's, out into the street. He was looking for something but Manjit was unsure exactly what it was.

The boys drank up and decided to head off to a more happening and livelier venue. Their chosen spot was merely across the road. They all made their way eagerly.

They staggered across the road to a newly opened bar next to the Treaty Centre – *'The Masala Beer Factory.'* They looked through the window and it was enough to set the pulse of these hapless warriors racing, as the bar was lined wall to wall with more sexy Asian girls then you could shake a stick at. There were some wearing mini skirts showing off their curvaceous legs, others with low cut tops and others next to nothing as they soaked up the early evening atmosphere on this hot and balmy August evening.

'Put it this way, any of you don't pull tonight then you are either gay or dead.' Gaurav laughed as he laid down the first ground rule for the evening. The gauntlet of trying to chat some girls up was thrown to the ground. (The gauntlet being a protective glove worn by medieval knights. It was said that knights would toss their glove to the floor when they wanted to cross swords with another knight. Then whatever knight picked up the gauntlet would mean they wished to fight).

Gaurav's words had an air of truth about them as the gang entered through the foyer and past the big, black and burly bouncers leading into the factory.

'Nah I am good – I will just watch you lot in action, and pick up some tips.' Saty joked back. 'What's that you womble?' Gaurav snorted as he turned to face him, face scrunched up.

'Oh look at the angel of moral rectitude, his halo just dropped off.' Gaurav had another swipe at Saty, further denting his confidence and depressing his spirit even more.

Hardeep and Manjit looked nervously at one another. There was tension in the air and for some reason all the signs were pointing towards the night ending in a fist fight with potentially dire consequences. Saty did not respond, wisely and they all entered the venue. The tension still lingering around them.

It appeared that sympathy was not on the menu today, only unreserved ball breaking and ribbing of the highest calibre.

'Oh and when we chat some birds up then if I get the one who is engaged or married or something, I am totally swapping with you bhanchods you feel me.' Gaurav was referring to the situation when an equal amount of guys meet a similar number of gals. It is a mere lottery which girl or guy that you all hone in to chat up. If your luck is out you will get the one who is happily engaged or married and that is the end of your evening with them.

On the other hand, your friend strikes lucky with the girl who just wants a one night stand, has been sexually deprived for the last fifteen years and through drinking seven shots of vodka thinks your goofy friend scrubs up like Brad Pitt. He ends up scoring and you get the BFH (bus fare home).

Once they went inside they bomb burst and Hardeep went off to one side of the bar where he was seen fumbling with his phone. It appeared as though he was listening to a voicemail message, whilst Saty went to the toilet. Manjit walked up to the bar to order a double order of beers for the guys along with a pitcher of sangria. The cool summer evening bringing with it a Mediterranean flavour. Gaurav headed off towards a crowd of giggling Asian girls where he immediately started to warm them up with his chat up lines. He was a seasoned veteran in this field and he knew that at least a couple of them would be sharing a hotel bed with him that evening.

After an hour or so of chatting and laughing and walking around The Masala Beer Factory, they were all very much drunk and in the full swing of the evening. Hardeep hinted at Manjit as they sat around chatting and harmlessly flirting with a couple of Asian girls they had snared earlier. 'I love her man...I feel lost. What do I do bro?' The drink making Hardeep more candid then he would have probably wanted to be as they chatted over the murmur of voices around them.

Manjit knew full well that this was his brother's way of justifying his sordid affair that he was having. They say the truth always spurts out when you are in your cups drinking. 'She is my world and I don't know what to do to make her love me again.' Hardeep's voice began to crack and fade. One of the Asian girls 'Kamljit' looked on in terror as the stud who had been chatting to her only a moment ago was now turning into a quivering and drooling wreck before her very eyes. She slinked away hastily before he started to blub like a big girl's blouse and soak her ensemble.

Manjit listened on concerned for his brother and deeply regretted the fact that he had slept with his brother's wife behind his back, he would do anything to turn the clock back as he would never intentionally dream of hurting him – NEVER!

Manjit also knew that his brother's extra marital liaison was the knock on effect of Raj being frosty towards him and their marriage hitting the rocks. Hardeep was just not the cheating type. He knew his brother too well and it was just not his style, but then again neither was he, and look what happened. It was obvious to Manjit that Hardeep was probably having comfort sex with some stranger to make up for the deficiencies in his relationship with Raj. He was also convinced that Raj's aloofness was probably caused by the fact that she had discovered the disease lurking within her system and this had triggered off their problems. These thoughts brought the situation firmly into sharp focus for him.

Over on the dance floor, Gaurav had a blonde gori in his arms. He was passionately kissing her. It was crazy; here they were on a supposed guy's night out when all he was concerned about was getting his own kicks with the local felines. This was all very good Saty thought to himself but why drag all of them along just so that he could spend the entire evening chatting up girls, it was one of his many bug bears about going out. This was beginning to irritate Saty as he observed Gaurav like a hawk from his vantage position in the beer garden.

Hardeep then got up to read a text message that he had just received. Manjit raised his eyebrows realising who it was from. Hardeep went over to the other side of the garden to read it as you do when you receive a normal routine text message. His behaviour bizarre, and giving veiled hints to the others that he was scratching on the surface of cheating on his wife; if not already doing so.

He was even seen smirking when he read it to himself in the distance. Saty leaned over to Manjit and whispered 'listen mate, what ever happened with you and that girl you were checking out before?'

'Nah nothing, I broke it off with her and that was that. She backed off. Never heard anything after that. 'A great white lie. Who was Saty? When he had easily lied to his wife for 3 solid months when he would make excuse after excuse.

Gaurav suddenly walked over with the tall and leggy gori held tightly with his arm draped around her shoulder and hugging his body tightly. 'Guys let me introduce you to Samantha.' Gaurav was grinning like a Cheshire cat as he had found his bed victim for the evening. Samantha smiled, her pretty red lipstick and fair skin being accentuated by the dusky evening light. She was good looking and the boys gave their look of approval. 'I am just going to the toilet babe, you ready to go when I return.' Her posh West London accent making their tails stand on end. She was not only a stunner, but was a posh stunner. 'Sure babe – I will be right here.'

Gaurav kissed her on the lips and she walked off back into the bar and towards the toilets, shaking her haunch at the pack of hounds as she sauntered off.

As soon as she turned her back, Gaurav spoke excitedly 'man she is one fit bitch. I am going to fucking ruin her tonight I swear, ride her like a Comanche, dabke dabke (he slammed his own fist into his open hand mimicking a fornicating action) and you know what they say about those posh girls in the sack.' He then clenched his fist tightly, the veins in his neck popping up in his delirium. 'Oh and I am single remember.' He reaffirmed his old and well rehearsed routine with his mate's. Saty just looked on pensively and Manjit smiled.

'Once you have bedded a girl of that calibre then perfunctory sex with the missus isn't the same, hey, but you gotta treat them like hookers in the sack, nothing more or they get all clingy.' He nudged Manjit in the ribs, spilling his pint. His behaviour was becoming more raucous and out of control by the minute, and typifying his incompetence in preventing his own marriage from going off the rails as it was daily. 'Oh yeah my clinging vine is probably sitting at Tej's house right now pining over me, ha. I'll sort her out afterwards.'

Gaurav continued in his outpouring of senseless garbage as Manjit listened on. 'She is good looking mate, well done.' Manjit was careful not to get too involved just in case Rita got a sniff of what he had been up to and asked him at a later date. 'Good looking, puh-lease. She is just a vessel man, a vessel to unleash my man fury on, you understand.' Gaurav thrust his hips forward drunkenly as he emphasised this.

Manjit however just nodded his head. He had the satisfaction of knowing that when he cheated it was not pre meditated initially and that small crumb of comfort was soothing. Hardeep returned to the group, he looked pleased with himself. Gaurav told him what was happening and Hardeep laughed. It was as if these cheaters were two peas in a pod, as they carried on leading the kind of parasitical life that had once lured him away from his wife.

'Oi before you go you kunjar at least have a drink with us okay.' Hardeep whisked out a twenty and passed it over to him. 'Get some beers in and then we will send you on your way.' It was as if it was his suhaag raat they way they talked.

Gaurav walked inside and was seen telling Samantha that she would have to be kept on ice for another ten minutes while he had a cheeky community beer with the boys; she understood and went outside to join the boys at the table. Gaurav meanwhile strutted up to the bar like king cock. He was a chancer, a player and he was untouchable when it came to the girls. His rugged good looks like a magnet to the girls that the others could only have dreamed about having, and tonight he was about to lay an absolute corker, a blonde, leggy, fair skinned beauty, oh and posh to boot...nirvana and Christmas rolled into one night he thought.

Across the bar a set of eyes remained fixed on him as they had been all evening, the same eyes that had trailed him from the previous bar. Every twitch, every joke, and every girl he chatted up was being recorded. He was being monitored closely and now finally he was alone as the stranger made their way across the bar with a pint glass gripped tightly in their hand. Gaurav had no idea of the fury that lurked so near, so imminently around him, no idea at all...

—⁓—

CHAPTER 17

A peach

The stranger was by now a mere glassing distance away, an arm's length from despatching their prey. The pint glass twirled in sinister fashion in the assailants hand as they surveyed the final few seconds before the carnage unfolded before the happy revellers in the bar. Gaurav leant up on the bar, his arms folded casually and tapping his foot to the sound of the beat being emitted from the loud speakers. He glanced outside and noticed the group of nicotine addicts all huddled up near the entrance taking desperate drags from their dog ends and filling their lungs with poison. Gaurav shook his head and knew that was one vice that he had thankfully managed to steer clear of throughout his life, and especially as he regarded his body a temple with hordes of grateful worshippers around him.

The stranger moved forward impatiently as the bar area coincidentally began to empty with the victim Gaurav standing on his lonesome and in for a nasty surprise. Suddenly, Hardeep appeared through the double doors from the beer garden. He was holding his mobile phone pressed against his ear and was whispering in the phone. He walked quickly and furtively past Gaurav as he headed towards the entrance to the pub 'yeah I will see you in a second, I am just coming outside,' he whispered. Gaurav raised his eyebrows and smirked as his laser focussed friend ambled past him.

The stranger stepped back and shuffled stealthily to their original position at the end of the bar. The pint glass was returned to the bar top and for the time the pervading atmosphere of hostility and demise returned to its status quo of fun and binge drinking.

The curvaceous bar lady then deposited the pints of Cobra beer and Malibu and coke in front of Gaurav. He handed over a crisp twenty pound note and then carried pints over to the revellers outside. He returned and repeated the process with all the drinks this time. Samantha was making small talk with the guys in the beer garden. Saty sat there stunned and patently intoxicated by her aesthetic magnificence whilst Manjit kept stealing surreptitious looks at her breasts from her plunging neck line, and who could blame them, she was a stunner.

'Where's Hard's got to?' Manjit asked the others, his eyes having a quick look around the beer garden. 'He went outside to meet someone I think, well that's what I heard him say.' Gaurav chipped in. Saty and Manjit looked at each other quizzically whilst Gaurav stroked Samantha's silky thigh up and down with his hand. The waves of pleasure stampeding through his system and keeping the old drinking nemesis, *'brewers droop,'* well at bay.

'Let me go and see if he is alright.' Manjit stood up and walked back into the bar and through the entrance of the pub, past the smoker's corner and into the street searching for his brother. A pair of eyes followed his every move, hands twitchy and breath shallow. The stranger was in a good vantage position studying the precise movements of the group whilst remaining undetected.

Outside Manjit scanned the environment for clues as to where his brethren had disappeared. He was nowhere to be seen and had vanished if Gaurav's recollection about him being outside was in fact true he thought. Suddenly he saw something in the distance, heads moving. He looked closely and through the rear window of a racing green Ford Fiesta, he noticed his brother sat in the passenger seat apparently chatting away freely to what looked like a female who was sat teasingly next to him in the drivers seat. Manjit's mouth opened wide on shock. He looked closely even craning his head down to ensure his eyes were not deceiving him. There they were cavorting as he had suspected, the female driver turned her head sideward's towards Hardeep and they shared a long and lingering look, the sort of look you give your partner just before you lean in for the kiss.

Suddenly the female driver looked around through the car window; her timing was impeccable as Manjit hurled himself behind a nearby wall in combat fashion to maintain his cover. In that split second he recognised her as being the same girl from the coffee shop that day, the one who was being chatted up by his brother. His reactions were sublime and the female driver looked back at Hardeep, her suspicions removed immediately as she looked down the soulless street. Manjit meanwhile dusted himself down and slowly regained his footing, he breathed a sigh of relief as he had not quite been picked out of the line up for being a sick, perverted peeping tom and his voyeuristic kicks had been masked on this occasion.

He looked back at the car, peeping around the corner with only his eyes and nose peering into the street, the remainder of his body like a cartoon illustration slanted horizontally behind the wall. The lovers were still sat there and it was as plain as a samosa is a triangular shaped pastry that they had been snogging like a couple of long lost sweethearts. Hardeep got out of the car and looked over both shoulders as he done so; after all he didn't want to be seen by anyone did he. Manjit remained hidden and pressed up against the wall. It was clear that he had watched far too many Bollywood movies as a youngster and in true Rajesh Khanna style nodded his head up and down as the truth of his earlier suspicions was confirmed before his very eyes; his brother was also having an affair behind his wife's back.

Manjit stood there nodding his head slowly absorbing what he had witnessed, the cold facts of the encounter, as Hardeep flashed past him across the street

Once Hardeep had returned within the venue Manjit followed suit and entered after him. Hardeep walked into the beer garden first and a few seconds Manjit appeared behind him. 'Kidda, where you been? I have been looking for you,' Manjit asked.

'Oh I went to the toilet, had the shits.'

'What for 15 minutes?' Manjit teased him. Hardeep looked at his brother, his eyes squinting, it was clear that with the drink flowing that Manjit was setting him up for something and he didn't like the sound of what was on the horizon. Manjit had his own visor down and for the sake of personal future insurance of his previous affair wanted to ask his brother the squirming questions that had bloodbath scrawled all over them.

'Yeah and since when do you shit in someone's car then hey?' The knee buckling question was thrown out there in it's gory detail.

Hardeep spun around quickly, angry and feeling betrayed. Like Michael Corleone had said once in the Godfather films - 'never take side's against the family, never.' The bustle and terror of the evening air started to descend upon them, but the drink only helped to fuel their bravado.

Yet here was a brash and arrogant Manjit asking him to justify what he was doing having an extra marital affair in front of his friends, this was a cheap stunt, but Manjit for all his ills had his motives, one word swirled around in his head – INSURANCE!

Hardeep stuttered for a second, he picked up a pint glass as all eyes bore into him waiting for his response; even Gaurav was distracted from the luscious beauty of his bed babe for a second as he too concentrated his look on the sinking rat Hardeep.

Hardeep's mind was in overdrive as he composed his deceitful response and cover up. He was not sure of how much the group knew so thought best to tease them with snippets of information so that the situation and facts could be assessed as he rambled on. 'A friend owed me some money so I told them to meet me here, it is no big deal.'

'How much money?' Saty doing his best impression of Laurel with his inquisitive stoking of the fire at such an apt moment in the proceedings.

Manjit looked at his brother with a look of surprise and sadistic pleasure as he feebly attempted to conceal his affair from the clan. It was evident that the brothers were from the same blood line, as they both knew the wily tricks to fight valiantly from their fox holes when on the ropes with an incriminating line of questioning about their illicit trysts.

Hardeep continued in his Oscar winning performance muttering a few conversational conjunctions about his outstanding debt. At one stage, assisted with the copious amounts of booze slushing in his liver, he opened his jacket showing the tip of a folded brown envelope. 'There...that is the dosh in there...now fuck off you bhanchod's.'

He pointed to an envelope that he had coincidentally and luckily left in his inner jacket pocket and showed the guys, hoping in vain to slake their imminent and insatiable urge to pin him to the pub wall and lynch him. It worked as they all settled down and laughed it off, his serendipity in finding the envelope had called the bloodhounds off the scent, and that night he would rest easy with his secret safely ensconced in the darkest and most perverse depths of his brain.

Hardeep turned to Manjit and said 'hey bro are you looking forward to the game?' He was referring to the tickets they had for the football match in Liverpool tomorrow. 'Yeah really up for that, it will be mad. I reckon we will stuff United' he replied.

Samantha turned to Gaurav after the commotion had died down and whispered a sweet nothing in his ear that in turn plastered a devilish grin all over his face. Her soft breath caressing the inside of his ear canal and her perfume lingering seductively. She was profuse in her intentions and it seemed that his quest for lust for the evening was a mere taxi ride away, if indeed the lovebirds even made it out of the taxi such was the elec-trifying chemistry that was being openly flouted in front of his comrades.

Gaurav stood up, shook the legs of his jeans down, and flipped the bottoms back over his shoes, even a quick visit to the toilet was an all important escapade, and he had to look the mutts nuts at every opportunity. 'Back in a minute gorgeous.' He winked at Manjit. 'Oh and I'll see you in a minute too Samantha.' The group laughed, good looking and funny, you could see why Samantha was creaming her knickers just at the thought of this wolf trying to tame the rampant tigress that she was becoming as every second ticked.

Gaurav turned and walked into the main area of the pub, slowly easing himself past the revellers who had began to stuff themselves into the cramped bar area. It was a sticky evening and there was a wild mob salivating at the thought of a frothy ice cold beer hitting their charred and chafing lips. They all wielded crisp ten and twenty pound notes in front of their noses trying to entice the hapless bar staff to dance to their drinking tune. Gaurav smirked at their menacing cursing under their breath as the bar staff went about their business with the reactions of diseased and paralysed slugs. Gaurav made it to the doors leading into the toilet and went straight to the urinals where he relieved himself with glee.

As he finished he went over to the wash basin and washed his hands with a dash of soap and water. He flicked the remnants of water onto his hair and greased it down over his skull admiring himself in the mirror. He turned and sized up the condom vending machine cling-ing to the wall at the far end of the toilet and beckoning him to it with a curled index finger. He strolled over whilst fishing in his pockets for some change that he duly slotted into the coin dispenser, *ribbed for extra pleasure – yes ma'am,* he thought as the pack of three fell to the holding tray after the depression of a couple of buttons. He scooped up the box, stuffed it into his rear pocket, and walked past the mirror, stopping to preen his hair once more before launching himself back into the arena of the pub and thirsty folk.

He once again walked past the swathe of people milling around like lost sheep. The music booming from the speakers deafening him as he negotiated his way through towards the doors leading into the beer garden when suddenly – THUD!

Gaurav staggered back a few feet as the victim of a thundering and rib rattling shoulder barge. The kind you used to get in the school playground by the local bullies intent on then dragging you into the toilets and pulling your teeth out with pliers (alright – my school was like the Bronx).

Gaurav quickly composed himself and looked up in the direction of the push, he had not quite fallen to the ground but found himself in a weird kind of crouched ski-ing position. He straightened up and stepped forward his fist clenched and body egged on by the booze as he quickly searched for his quarry. All he saw was a smattering of jovial bodies moving and hustling about in front of him. He unclenched his fists and calmed down, it was only an accident he thought. He would be damned if he would let a minor skirmish interfere with his plans to bone his gori queen tonight.

Gaurav smiled and quickly waded through the remaining guys finally making it into the summer freshness of the beer garden, leaving the alcohol flea pit behind him in great fashion. He took hold of Samantha's arm and wrenched her up from her seat 'come on treacle it is about time you and me grease the wheels of our relationship.'

'Give me a moment just going to powder my nose, haramzada.' Samantha responded bravely.

Manjit almost fell over the table laughing as his wind up had worked according to plan.

'What did you say?' Gaurav incredulous turned to face Samantha, half grinning. 'I am sorry he told me to say that, what does it mean, sorry he said it means sexy...you bastard.' She directed her curses to Manjit who chortled heartily.

Saty looked up at Gaurav and cast him a disapproving and disregarding look, his friend's skulduggery with his wife not scoring any brownie points with him.

Saty turned to Manjit, his dearest confidant, and whispered 'don't you just hate that?'

'What's that bro?' Manjit looked sideward's at him, whilst Gaurav took a call on his mobile at that moment and moved to one side and out of earshot for a few seconds.

Saty continued 'just that we are meant to be out with the boys, you know a boys night and at the first sniff of getting his leg over he wanders off and ditches us, that SUCKS!'

Saty emphasised the word with vehement passion that caused Manjit to move his head back. The main cause of his sudden jolt backwards being from the missile of saliva that the wolf boy had spat into his eye as he enunciated *sucks.'*

Manjit wiped the saliva from his eye, with a curious vision of having to speak to his friend behind a shower curtain in future meetings making him chuckle to himself as the last traces of soggy spittle was finally removed from his eye and flicked to the floor and wiped on his jeans. Hardeep meanwhile looked on, his face plastered with worry and deep in cogitation. It was clear that he had brushed with chance a few moments ago when he was given the Spanish Inquisition over his disappearing act with his mistress. He looked fraught with worry, hoping to himself that word of his liaison would not leak and frame him in the following morning papers as the Hardeepgate scandal.

Suddenly a voice was heard next to Gaurav 'she taste's like a peach doesn't she?' The three seated guys looked up at the direction of the voice as it was clear that it was focussed in on the group's conversation and interaction. A group of guys stood next to their table, maybe it was a misunderstanding, and they were talking amongst themselves.

'And a good kisser too...' The voice continued to tease the group as it boomed over again.

'What's that mate?' Gaurav asked the stranger standing next to him, and very much invading his private circle, I mean any closer and they would have been dancing the Tango around the beer garden.

'No I am just saying that she is the most succulent peach I have tasted...ever!' The voice came back, the stranger turned to face Gaurav, his nostrils flaring. DAMN! It had to be Samantha's estranged lover, her husband, her brother (no not her brother that is sick unless she was a pervert). Gaurav studied the stranger for a second, he had not seen him before, and neither had the other guys.

'Okay do I know you?' Gaurav asked confidently opening his stance up, a clear sign that when someone does this, i.e. stands there with their fists dangling by their side and with an open stance, then they do not regard you as a threat. It was an old fighter's trick and the stranger was being sucked in.

'Nah you don't know me.' The stranger replied nonchalantly. The stranger was Amar, the guy who had been watching the group all evening, the one who had contemplated 'glassing' Gaurav, the guy who had shoulder barged him just minutes earlier and now he was ready for the kill.

'Then do you know Sam?' Gaurav asked, his voice gruff and irritated at the presence of this imbecile, the scamp who was intent on being a smart arse after a few too many sherbets.

'Nah, don't know her either.' Amar mocked him and before Gaurav could respond continued his slurring insults. 'Like I said she is a peach...your wife...when I went down on her at work, a peach.' Amar had thrown his hat into the ring as he stepped forward from the group, the teasing and mocking replaced with a vicious hostility. Pellets of sweat gushed down the forehead of Gaurav as the reality of the situation rapidly came to fruition.

'What did you say about my wife?' Gaurav took a step back, lining himself up for a Vinod Mehra swinging punch aiming at Amar's hanging Desperate Dan chin hanging their invitingly like a camel's bollock.

'Teri maa de phudi...(your mum's nether regions) you fuck around and then you give it my wife this, my wife that, bhanchod kuta.' Little dribbles of spittle started to foam and appear on the bottom lip of Amar.

Manjit, Hardeep and even Saty quickly stood up, a look of fear plastered on their faces. The one thing that any good street fighter will tell you is to forget the trading of insults, forget the chest puffing and scowling looks; NO! The most important thing for self preservation is to check the adversaries hands, is he tooled up? Does he have the curtain falling weapon in his mitts that will send you on a one way ticket to the crematorium and will have your Dad crashing to his knees at your wasted young life as he reads out your epitaph at your funeral?

Gaurav snarled back at Amar 'yeah what you gonna do? You taken the Matrix pill or something you tosser?' His hectoring voice booming across the garden. Well in this situation, Gaurav had mistimed his opponent's desire and more importantly failed to notice the knuckleduster that suddenly and ferociously came careering towards his face. Gaurav saw the swing too late. He tried to duck but it was over, as the full thunderous and unrelenting force of the knuckleduster and punch smashed straight into his nose.

The cartilage and bridge of his nose deserted him as it bomb blasted all over his face, sending the searing and shooting pain straight to his brain. Amar was not finished as he followed up with a flurry of stampeding kicks and punches all over Gaurav whilst he was pulled of by the Asian guys standing next to him and the futile efforts of Manjit and Hardeep. Saty just looked on, completely frozen with fear, the adrenaline sucking any movement out of his body as he stayed rooted firmly to the spot as though his feet had been impaled into the ground.

Gaurav took a beating without as much as a retaliatory fist raised in defence. His fight was left in the sandbox as soon as he opened his stance in such a school boy manner, and especially against an unknown nemesis, an angry, determined and tooled up nemesis. He stood not a snowball in hell's chance of surviving the encounter with at least something dislodged or broken. As soon as Amar was prised off Gaurav, almost crowbar like, he shouted 'now you fucker I am going to get what's mine.' No sooner had he said that, he darted out of the rear entrance and into the night. The boys sat Gaurav down and supplies of napkins were handed to him by a nearby Florence Nightingale customer.

Gaurav sat there his thoughts in a whirl 'what happened?' He had been savagely attacked by a big and brawny brute of a man whom he had never met before. It just seemed surreal. He was concussed and dabbed at his nose. It resembled a pakora as it flipped about his face, scrunched and squashed from the force of the punch. The pain still real but cleverly being disguised with the drink, adrenaline and shock. 'What did he mean get what's mine?' He babbled, looking up at his stunned friends. Gaurav had been caught in the rough terrain of affairs tonight but his thoughts immediately receptive to the clue that his assailant had dropped before he escaped into the darkness of the night.

They returned concerned but blank looks to his question. The remaining patrons in the garden slowly began to return to their circles and continue drinking, slavishly entertained with the blood sport for the evening. The bouncers however were totally incognizant to the dissention in the garden as were the majority of revellers in the bar area. The one sided rumpus was over within three seconds and the suspect had left the scene a few seconds after that.

'What did he mean, does he know my wife or something?' Gaurav's voice became more desperate.

Samantha suddenly appeared by his side, her open jawed expression making all of them look up at her. 'You shit bag.' She threw the contents of a nearby pint glass over his face causing him to reel back from the shock of the icy beer along with the sudden jolt of his nose cartilage as it clung on by the tiniest of fibres in his nostril. 'What's that for, I am the...'

Samantha cut in 'you didn't tell me you were married? I just heard you asking about your wife, you cheating scumbag, go to hell.' With that she stormed past the slowly gathering crowd as they nestled back into their ring side seats for round two of the evenings cabaret.

Meanwhile, Amar had called Rita on the mobile and pulled up outside Tej's house. He then went into meticulous detail about the war story, crucially omitting the bit involving the knuckle duster, he didn't want to scare her off, not after she was being carefully reeled in on his rod. Rita walked out of the house and jumped into his car and a deep and meaningful conversation took place.

'Babe you have to leave him today. If you don't then this is it for me, I can't stand for you to be wasted on someone like him.' The tears rolled down her cheeks, she looked down at her wedding ring as Amar reiterated the fact that he was about to screw some blonde bimbo had he not intervened. The wedding ring gently slipped off her finger.

'Okay, I need to pick up some stuff from my flat then I will stay at yours until I can sort my head out with what's happened this evening.' With that Amar squeezed her hand and his eyes softened; a look that told her many things. His parents were in India and this made the situation easier for her to regroup her thoughts and direction in life should she decide to stay at his house for the time, that decision was not fait accompli as Amar drove off.

The most important thing was that she was worshipped by Amar, and that was all she had hoped for ever since she played mummies, daddies, and weddings as a little girl.

Over at the scene of the brawl Gaurav suddenly sprung to his feet discarding the napkins to the floor 'quick get a taxi, we have to get to my flat, something is up...I am being screwed.' He darted across the beer garden and into the rear street. He sprinted to a nearby unlicensed taxi and began to open the door to the back as the other three raced after him also piling into the taxi with him. One thing was certain – the night was far from over and the *'masala was only just being sprinkled'*...

CHAPTER 18

—⁓—

Fat lady sings

The taxi ploughed down Staines Road eventually screeching to a deafening halt outside Gaurav's flat, the boys being tossed around like balls in a lottery machine in the back despite having their seat belts on. Hardeep was about the only one still intact as he had the sensibility to sit in the front on his own.

Gaurav flung himself out of the car like a cheetah on anabolic steroids heading towards the communal door with a sedulous look in his eyes that the other three amigo's had never seen to this day. He was pursed by the others as Manjit tossed a £10 note on the drivers lap from his position in the back as he too scrambled out in his bid to halt the tsunami that was his friend.

Gaurav suddenly slowed down as he approached the front door of his flat, it was slightly ajar, and he could hear rummaging inside along with faint whispering voices. He tentatively paced up to the door, his ears tuned acutely in to the furtive conversation that was taking place within his very own castle.

Suddenly his friends came scuttling up the stairs with frantic expressions on their faces. Gaurav moved his hand up and down with his lips curled up telling them to quieten down, they responded immediately like obedient kutay, sensing his urgency with his hand movements. If all else failed in his life he had a guaranteed job as a dog trainer. I bet if he held up a burning hoop they would all bound up and through it with their wet tongues curled and hanging out from the side of their mouths. Gaurav had a prepared fusillade of questions that he needed answers to from his wife but now there were developments, voices scheming and planning inside his flat and he listened closely.

'Come on we just have to go, pick this stuff up when things have calmed down, he is hot right now.' The voice from within was none other than the knuckle dusting wielding bandido Amar addressing Rita. Here he was with all his temerity and balls drinking water from the well that was Amar's home and wife. Gaurav had heard enough and gritted his teeth pushing the door wide open and stepping inside, his thoughts skewered from the disturbing events of the evening. Amar swivelled around and glared at Gaurav, his face serious and uncompromising. Rita gasped as she stood there clutching a carrier bag tightly with both hands. Manjit, Hardeep and Saty appeared around Gaurav all staring in disbelief at the unfolding situation. Gaurav looked into the eyes of his wife and then back again at Amar, his nostrils flared and nose drooping to one side and still throbbing from the earlier pounding.

'So what you doing with my wife?' Manjit stuck his arm across the chest of Gaurav as he spoke to prevent him from hurling himself into another guaranteed beating as the veins in Amar's forearms began to appear from the surge of adrenaline in his body.

'Look pal, it is over, this is a two way street.' Amar cut straight to the point 'ask her if you don't believe me.' Amar glanced at Rita for affirmation, who was sobbing into her hand. She did not want to end her marriage this way, in such circumstances, with an audience and more importantly with green snot trickling down through her fingertips.

Gaurav searched for some kind of response across the loom of his imagination. His stomach churned with the sickening reality of his wonderful wife, his beautiful princess walking out of his life for some knuckle scraping thug as he fought hard not to sink to his knees and whimper like a baby with his thumb in his mouth. Thoughts of them sleeping together and '*doing it*' torturing his soul and raping his senses.

He felt emasculated as Rita spoke through her sobbing lamentations and increasingly anxious whining 'it is over, you have broken my heart.' There was a stunned silence as the four friends stood there at the entrance to the flat totally dumbfounded as to what they were witnessing, none more so than Gaurav.

'Look mate you shouldn't mess with someone else's wife, it is not fair.' Amar shifted his eyes across to Saty as he attempted to stick up for and salvage the situation for his friend, despite the earlier problems that they had been having. Saty's overwhelming sense of fair play had the better of him coupled with four beers, and now he was ready to rumble with the Devil himself such was his valour. Even Gaurav looked around at his friend's bravery, whilst Amar cast him a look of contempt, dismissing the comment as you would brush off a bit of fluff on your sleeve. 'You sure you have enough insulation there (referring to the hair sprouting out up and above the tee shirt he was wearing) shouldn't you be out there on your quest for fire or something?'

His jaundiced remarks intimating that Saty was the most direct link to a hairy Neanderthal as they had seen in the millennium. His deft retort shattering his attempted charm campaign swifter than a kick to the ghoulies as Saty slinked back behind the others with not so much as a squeak.

'Now we don't want a scene, just let us go and you two can sort this situation out later when things have calmed down.'

Amar spoke with an air of sanctimonious repulsion as he slowly walked closer to Gaurav and the others, his left hand now tightly holding on to Rita's left hand as he ushered her along with him past her husband.

Rita sidled up close to Amar clutching his hand tightly. She sought solace in the fact that their marriage had been over, dead and buried the first time she had caught her philandering husband cheating on her many moons ago. His deeply unsettling actions throughout their relationship had culminated in this moment when she let go of Amar's hand suddenly and stretched her hand out to Gaurav as she approached him.

Gaurav's eyes lit up like a Christmas Tree, maybe she had come to her senses, maybe they could give it one more try with a fresh slate. His heart pounded even harder against his chest as their hands met. Saty stood erect and looked down his nose at Amar as it appeared the couple were rekindling their love. Their hands touched and the wave of ecstasy swept through Gaurav's body, the ruinous consequences of the situation now about to be forgotten as she had chosen her husband over her fancy man. He gripped her hand harder and attempted to slowly pull her in to him, she leant in and reciprocated the squeezing of hands before suddenly pulling away and slowly moving backwards, her eyes streaming with a waterfall of soggy tears.

Gaurav felt a lurch in his heart as he opened his hand in front of him and there it lay; the slayer of truth and damning evidence that the fat lady had sung her last note. Their wedding ring sizzled in his palm and seemed to bore it's way through his skin, into his veins and straight into his heart, the jagged edges of the diamonds piecing through his pericardium and twisting further into the very depths of his ticker like a frenzied lathe machine. The fact was that there was another suitor out there who could slice a better cheddar than him, who could love 'his' girl as he could not.

Amar took hold of Rita's hand again and gently pulled her out with him through the door and down the stairs to his waiting car. Manjit and Hardeep could do nothing but stare; it was not their place to get involved. They merely had to provide a support framework for their mate and besides none of them fancied a knuckle duster on their hooters. The couple left the building with Rita's sobs still heard from the stairwell as they vanished out of sight. Gaurav made a last ditch desperate lunge for his wife, but it was too little and too late as she vanished. Rita had earlier told Amar that she was not about to get involved with him until such time as she had straightened her head out, to which he was acquiescent.

Gaurav looked over his shoulder, it was over, and she was gone. He paused, his body wallowing in a sea of self pity and then slowly walked over to the sofa flopping his limp and weary body down. His wife had fallen for this mystery guy, someone who had a faster lick. The guys quickly sat around him trying to console him. He lay down horizontal and rested his arms over his head as the tears stung his eyes like pin pricks in his eyeballs. This magnet for the chica's had been eviscerated through his sheer over indulgence. He knew that he had been the author of his own misfortune it was as simple as that.

The boys remained with their fallen brethren for another hour after the watershed in his life patching up his spirits with banter and other such sympathetic talk. It worked as he eventually sat up and engaged in mindless conversation with all of them.

'Bruv, we are gonna skedaddle…you gonna be cool if we go?' Manjit asked him gently, his hand on his shoulder and squeezing down softly. 'Yeah yeah I am okay now. This shit was on the cards for ages, I just didn't expect it to explode in my face like it did tonight.' He looked down frowning and studying the wedding ring that he had brought his wife when they married, deep in thought, as he continued to twirl it between his finger and thumb.

The guys then slowly started to stand up and said their goodbyes. Hardeep called for a taxi from his mobile phone, 5 minutes was the response telling them to wait outside. Manjit and even Saty hugged Gaurav. Their support was welcoming and a much needed tonic after the events that had unfolded before their very eyes this evening. They walked out into the hallway of his flat. As the boys began to leave, Saty turned to Manjit 'is he going to be okay? I mean this is heavy?'

'Trust me that bloke is like a cockroach, he would survive anything and still come out unscathed, he will be fine, just a bit bruised and battered…I think it is a timely lesson for all of us, hey, none more than me. I am just glad that I have put that part of my life away under lock and key.'

Manjit was lucid with his thoughts, with the drink making him loquacious.

Saty's face scrunched into a question mark 'what do you mean?'

Manjit looked back at Hardeep and then at Saty 'you know my secret?' He was careful that the look did not give anything away or make Saty suspicious that his mistress was his brothers wife.

Saty suddenly smiled acknowledging, he knew what Manjit was talking about, albeit not exactly what girl he was referring to. They walked out down the stairs and out into the warm evening air. Hardeep had remained on hand to offer Gaurav some parting words of wisdom to keep his pecker up in such a delicate situation. Gaurav shook Hardeep's hand vigorously and they parted.

The three guys outside stood there for no more than 2 minutes before a minicab came careering around the corner in a whizzing, skidding fashion that would have done any Starsky and Hutch fanatic proud. The Asian minicab driver hurtled towards them like a scud missile before screeching to an ear splitting halt directly under their snouts. One by one the taxi driver dropped them off at their respective houses, Hardeep first, then Saty and finally Manjit, but that was when things turned from bad to deplorably terrible than even he could have imagined. The malevolence of the night air hummed sadistically as he placed his foot out of the taxi on to the tarmac immediately outside his house. He stepped out of the car sucking in the night air, but unbeknown to him, there was something lurking in the shadows, an evil so vengeful and depraved that the only outcome tonight was the spilling of blood. Little did he know that he was walking the green mile up to his door…

—ᴍ—

Denizen

Manjit moved on up his path and towards his front door, the house key in his hand as he fumbled for a second in finding the keyhole; like any good horror film worth its salt. He finally inserted it and went to turn the key. CRACK!

He turned sharply, the sound of a small twig snapping in the large hedge and overflowing shrubbery engulfing the front of his house brought his senses back into sharp focus. He instinctively put his hands up to his midriff as he scanned around to see who this intruder was. His heart was banging like a dhol. Suddenly, the intruder revealed themselves. It was next door neighbours tabby cat. The little feline bastard he thought, it had scared the living shit out of him. 'Get lost,' he mumbled as he shooed the cat away with his hand. The poor beast fled for its life, desperate not to have it's neck snapped like the twig that had fallen before it.

Manjit then turned to reach for the key in the lock and placed his hand on it, when suddenly a figure appeared from the neighbours garden crossing over the low adjoining wall with relatively ease. She had been hiding on a perch of ground surrounded by verdant bushes and shrubbery. Manjit visibly gulped as his grip on the key weakened. Raj, stepped forward from the shrubbery, her face shone ghostly white in the glare of the nearby lamp. Her face was flush from the vast amounts of alcohol she had indulged in earlier.

Like a denizen in the night, an unrepentant soldier, she emerged from the shadows and walked straight towards. She was strangely wearing a long black over-coat considering the moist humidity of the evening. The coat held expertly together in the front by her hand. Manjit's face scrunched up into a discombulated mess as he fought hard to contemplate what was happening. He did not need this anymore, why could she not just leave him alone? All he ever wanted was to lead a good and honourable life with his wife and future kids.

No sooner had he tried to piece together his jumbled up thoughts when the lapels of the coat were thrust open a few inches away from him, his eyes like a cartoon character dangled out of his eyes on small springs and bounced up and down like a yo yo. He even began mumbling incoherently in some made up foreign language. Once his eyes popped back in their sockets he quickly studied the objet d art being presented to him on a plate. Raj was indeed starkers, her silky thighs gently pressed together and her body with more curves than Brands Hatch. She stood tantalisingly before him like the treacherous sex obsessed whore she was. Sinful de-bauchery her motivating factors as Manjit remained paralysed as he stood there watching with unblinking patience.

The coat was then pulled shut again 'now get inside and take me.' Her voice demanding and menacing.

Manjit regained his confidence and ability to speak rather than drool 'look we have been here before, you have got to be kidding...and you have got...HIV.'

Raj looked him up and down with disgust 'and I wonder where I got that from you gunjar. Look you can use these.' She reached into the coat pocket and threw a packaged condom at him, which he instinctively caught in his hands.

'Don't argue with me, or I will tell your wife all about us...NOW get inside.' She was demented, did she actually think that she would win Manjit back with her hard nosed approach? It was nonsensical.

'Look I am warning you...' Manjit asserted as he wagged his trembling finger towards her. He was scared stiff and knew that her unpredictability was her most terrifying weapon. He simply did not know what she was prepared to do next such was the tension in his body. 'Ha, you are about as fearsome as a pink fluffy bunny armed with a piece of lettuce, now get inside like a good boy.' Raj dismissed his threat with mocking simplicity.

Raj walked right up to him and reached behind him turning the key in the lock and pushing the door open, she then thrust her hands out and pushed Manjit into his own house. He stumbled and fell to the floor of his hallway and quickly stood up. A combination of him being tipsy, and a sucker push being the factors that made him topple he thought as he waited for her next attack. Once inside she lost her coat as it slipped down to her ankles and black criss crossed shoes. She mule kicked the door shut behind her and walked over to him grabbing him with a powerful clinch and yanking his head downwards and onto her pouting lips.

She kissed hard, with passion and a fury that managed to enslave him in her cloak of passion once again. He tried to pull away, it had been over that day in the office and there was no way he was ever going to cheat on his wife again. He knew he had made that mistake once before. He struggled to move his head away but she kept hold with all the force she could muster, they grappled for a moment, her nails now digging into his scalp and neck. Little trickles of blood began to appear on the tips of her fingers from the wounds in his neck as he slapped her several times in the face to deter this naked, crazy and rabid bulldog.

This was the last thing that he needed as he fought with lion heartedness in his bid to prohibit her iniquitous advances. This session was now quickly becoming the final nail in the coffin of marital integrity despite his desperate rebuffs.

They both fell back on to the stairs as she ripped and pawed at his belt trying to undo it and feed her hand through the gap in between the top and his midriff. He pulled back as another nail dug deeply into his torso making him yelp 'get off you bitch…leave me alone.' Raj undeterred sliced and scraped her nails up his chest scrunching his nipples with nut cracking power tugging them towards her causing tears to stream out of Manjit's eyes such was the pain.

Despite slapping her, Manjit did not want to use violence on a girl, he had always looked down on guys who hit their partners and so was desperately resisting the urge to punch this possessed demon in the mouth and end it all. Raj shuffled her head around his hands as he tried in vain to push her head back. This was not enough as she sunk her teeth into his left nipple and crunched down hard, her teeth in gritting lock jaw and virtually touching each other as the nipple remained wedged and bleeding profusely in between. He could never remember crying as painfully as he was doing at that moment then throughout his entire life as the shooting pain rattled his insides with no compromise or sympathy. His search for some kind of reprieve was rapidly consuming all his remaining energy.

'Please leave me now.' He pleaded with her. She let go of his nipple even spitting out a mouthful of hairs to the floor as he slumped back on the stairs, his body shaking and quivering in the most unfathomable pain imaginable. It was over, she had humiliated him as she had wanted and now there had to be closure on her warped desires for him he prayed as he clutched his bleeding nipple whilst crying inconsolably. Raj standing over him naked, drunk and demented. She laughed as she tasted and scooped up the blood on her bottom lip with her tongue. He watched her through the narrow slits his watery eyes had become still holding his nipple and watching the blood flow from it onto his jeans. His neck was stinging from the deep wounds that had been inflicted, he was messed up and his erstwhile lover's crudity and spite dangled over him like the termagant she was.

Raj leant down and picked up her coat. She put it on, ensuring the buckle was fastened in the front, and now hiding her modesty. Manjit was still hyperventilating as he looked on waiting for the witch to leave him to nurse his wounds, but he had calculated wrong again. Raj had tasted blood and fuelled by the drink wanted more. She reached into the inside of the jacket, produced a large knife, and waved it in front of his face. Manjit's eyes widened in despair, what the hell was she going to do now? Surely she had wounded him enough, what more did she want. His mind suddenly stopped as she knelt down and placed the tip of the knife on his groin and began to slowly inch her way upwards to his crotch. 'What would you do if I cut it off hey? At least then it would stop you spreading that virus wouldn't it and stop you cheating on your wife, what do you reckon, how about I cut it off?

'No, no please Raj, listen to me don't do anything stupid...please...I know maybe we can talk tomorrow in the morning, I will call you, we can do lunch.' His voice was desperate, his tone pleading and Raj merely brushed it off by shaking her head. 'You see nobody ever dumps me, you understand and what I can't have I will take it anyway.'

The entire colour drained from Manjit's face and he began to whimper grievously. He closed his eyes as Raj raised the knife, firming her grip up, her teeth gritted and face concentrated on what she was about to do. Manjit screamed 'nooooo!'

Suddenly a voice was heard outside the front door. It was the voice of his wife Kully who had also returned from the girls evening after calming down from her earlier fight with Raj. She turned the key in the door and was waving goodbye to the Asian taxi driver who insisted that he waited until she actually got into her house before disappearing into the darkness.

Raj looked up at the door and then back at Manjit. She reached into her pocket and threw something towards the direction of the door before darting into the kitchen and gently closing the door behind her, crouching in the shadows and listening. Manjit tried to identify what she had thrown but it fell into the darkest corner of the hallway and the moonlight reflecting though the front door window only shone on his weary frame. Too late! The door opened letting in the ray of moonlight across his face and now a whole cornucopia of new problems had presented themselves...

Chapter 20

--- ⁓ ---

Impeccable timing

Kully opened the door and immediately saw the dishevelled and despairing figure of her husband laying half on the stairs and half on the floor. 'What the hell happened to you?' she enquired.

Manjit had not thought through any excuses. He wanted to desperately tell his wife how silly he had been and what agony he was in but he lowered his top and played it cool, promising himself that as soon as he got rid of the fiendish bitch in the kitchen he would confess everything about his affair. He decided that it would be best for her to know so that he could vow on his future progenies lives that if he ever strayed again then he would throw himself off a cliff. He loved Kully and this had been a steep and very painful learning curve as his nipple throbbed through his shirt.

Kully looked at him from the door 'is that blood?' she pointed to the red stain on his jeans. The moonlight straining past her and bouncing off his face.

Manjit looked down 'yeah I got into a fight, I got jumped in the pub. I promise I will tell you everything once I get myself sorted, I promise, I need to tell you something else too.' The overwhelming guilt of the entire sordid affair was brimming under the surface and ready to burst out into the open.

'Yeah I need to ask you something that I heard as well.' Her face became serious despite her intoxicated state. Her words seemingly disregarding any pain that her husband was in from the injuries inflicted in his 'pub fight.'

'I heard something today about you sleeping around. Tell me that it is just lies?' She looked him straight in the eyes and waited patiently for the truth. The suspicion looming over him regarding his faithless behaviour belying her reproachful questioning.

The catalyst for her questions being the fight with the very girl lurking surreptitiously only a few feet from her behind a closed door. Manjit hesitated and for some god forsaken reason felt compelled to divert his eyes across the hallway and at the object that Raj had discarded. Why he did this? Only he will ever know, and in years to come he will kick himself for this error in judgement. Kully twisted her head to see what he was searching for, and why he had felt the need to look when she had asked him the sixty four million dollar question.

There it was the evidence, a pair of red silky knickers. The pair Raj had knowingly tossed, hoping upon hoping that they would be unearthed in dramatic fashion. Kully placed her hand on her chest as she stooped down and picked them up. She looked over at her husband. He had cheated on her, he was nothing more than dirt on her shoe. Any shred of morality was dead and buried for an eternity in that one fleeting moment.

Manjit sat there looking back speechless and like a grilled mackerel. He knew his wife and she was reasonable, the kind of girl who would not resort to violence to resolve an issue. *(If only he had seen her in action a few hours ago, he may have thought twice)* He picked himself up and limped over to her 'look I need to get this off my chest and I didn't want you to find out like this, but babe two things.'

He stood in front of her and continued 'I love you so much and never want to lose you. Look we need to discuss this upstairs and I promise if you hear me out you will understand what has been going on.' His words carried a sense of purpose and conviction. Kully once more looked down at the red knickers that were dangling in her hand and then up at Manjit still in state of utter shock. Her foundations were crumbling around her. WHACK! BANG! SMASH! She viciously launched into a relentless assault of punches and kicks as they rained in from every conceivable angle.

Manjt cowered to the floor as he was set upon in a frenzy that would have even made Raj proud, her kicks landing several times to his exposed nipple as he scrunched his body up in searing pain. 'Bastard, cheater, kuta. How could you do that to me? I thought we were supposed to be different, tight like a unit, a team.' THUD! KICK! Her fury continued to erupt at her felled quarry, at one stage, she caught him flush in the knackers as his balls almost shot up and out of his mouth such was the ferocity. So much for being the non violent and understanding type.

'That is it – WE ARE OVER! YOU HEAR ME! OVER! OVER! HARAMZADA! Kully threw the silky knickers at his head, her suspicions of him being over the side with Raj had been confirmed. She raced upstairs and into the bedroom where she began to scoop up her belongings. Manjit managed to sit up and prop himself up against the bottom of the stairs, his head dizzy from the beatings he had taken. He could hear his wife calling for a taxi to take her to her parent's house.

At that moment, the kitchen door opened and Raj appeared in her black coat, knife still by her side. She stood over him mockingly and with a wry smile. 'Now with her out of the way, maybe we can finally be together' she whispered. Manjit looked up at her confused as to her diminishing mental state. Raj then walked out quietly through the front door and away she went. Several minutes later Kully came thundering down the stairs, she was holding a couple of bags and crying inconsolably. She brushed past her husband, opened the front door dumping her bags in the front garden, and then raced into the kitchen where she gulped down a pint of water. She was still shaking and crying as the last vestige of her marriage came crashing down around her feet. They say it takes years to build trust in a marriage and a second to destroy it.

Manjit limped to the kitchen in an attempt to confess 'please my darling, don't leave me…you don't know how much I love you, I will die for you, I promise I would. If I can't be with you then I have nothing.' His lip was quivering and words full of remorse. He meant it and begged for her forgiveness 'please Kully you are my life, don't leave me like this. I will tell you everything.'

She sobbed and walked out. Manjit tried to stop her 'baby please stop.'

Kully, her face flushed with hatred 'you can tell Joe, tell him everything because when he hears about this you know what he will do to you. Now get out of my way.' She brushed past him catching a sight of the taxi pulling up outside the address. 'I am going to KILL YOU for what you have done to me.'

Manjt hobbled up behind her, the pain from his testicles amongst other places excruciating. 'No, don't tell your brother, babe. He will go crazy, please at least do that much for me. Kully stopped half way down the path and turned to look back at him. Manjit's face lit up in anticipation and hope.

They both knew that one word to Joe and the result would not be pleasant for him.

'Too late I told him on the phone upstairs before I called the taxi' her voice hanging in the air with a twinge of guilt. She shook her head and walked away into the taxi, and like a mirage she disappeared before him, his eyes felt like they were being stung by bees such was the hollowness in his body. Her words trampling over his diminishing will to live.

His last glimmer of salvation had been ripped from his body, the beating heart of his marriage gone. He could take no more and someone was going to pay…

CHAPTER 21

—∽—

Broad Shoulder's

Manjit walked back inside disconsolate and heart broken. The virtues of marriage had been tragically slain and expunged from his life. He picked up his mobile phone and called Gaurav to share the misery that he too was facing on the very same evening as his brethren. After a few rings his friend answered 'kidda Manj what's up bro?' his voice deflated and hag ridden.

'Kully has walked out on me, she has left me...I feel so shit man. I messed up bro, I messed it all up for what?' Manjit was descending into a grievous lament before Gaurav snapped some reality back into the situation 'what's going on? I don't understand, what do you mean she has left you? What has happened? Have you two had a fight?' It was clear to both of these warriors that there was indeed something in the evening air as both their relationships were extinguished in one foul swoop, a mere coincidence, but nevertheless this dark cloud had appeared without compassion.

'It is too long to go into now. It is too messy but...I just wanted to know how you are feeling? Have you heard anything from Rita? Has she returned for her stuff or anything?' Manjit stood in the kitchen as his free hand searched the cupboard for the strongest pain killers he could lay his hands on. He needed something as it felt as though someone had taken a sledgehammer to both sides of his head, along with his throbbing nipple, such was the ball breaking pain.

There was a long pause and Manjit could hear whispering and giggling in the background, the sounds of a female chortling. 'What's that noise?' Manjit pressed the receiver closer to his ear to identify the noise.

'Oh nothing, I just asked Tanya from my gym to come over to keep me company and help me cope and all that.' He replied back. Manjit was flabbergasted by his friend's nonchalant attitude to his marriage break up; I mean here was Manjit suffering the full brunt of his sacrosanct marriage exploding in his face and there was Gaurav who had just suffered the same fate and was frolicking with a voluptuous girl from his gym.

Manjit knew very well what he meant by keeping him company and helping him cope. These euphemisms were easily decipherable.

'Okay I guess you are coping okay, listen take it easy and I will catch up with you later, I think we need to talk.' Manjit fought back the tears desperately as they said their goodbyes and terminated the call respectively. Gaurav went back to being soothed by his gori bit on the side from the gym while Manjit's eyes focussed back on the task, to eradicate his headache for the last time. He continued to rummage in the kitchen cupboards; he was feeling emasculated and so alone. His hand finally touched the top of a pill bottle as he drew it closer to him. The pain was still searing relentlessly throughout his aching body and soul.

It was without a label but he knew it had to be headache pills. Suddenly the phone rang; he quickly opened the pills and emptied three out on the palm of his hand before shoving the pills in his mouth and swallowing. He ran the tap and slurped a gallon full of water with his head bent down and tilted to one side, the good old fashioned way. The phone continued to ring on the table and then cut off. Manjit walked over to the other side of the kitchen and poured himself a generous home shot of Bacardi Black, about half a glass full. As he lifted the tumbler to his lips ready to sink the devilish brew, the phone crackled back into life, blaring out the acoustic version of Safri Boys Rahe rahe jaan valiye. Manjit quickly finished off the drink and walked over to the ringing phone. He picked it up and looked at the caller Id. His eyes were dazed and blurry from the effects of the drink along with the ferocious beating he had survived.

It was his brother; he looked across at the clock on the microwave. The time 10 minutes past midnight. He took the call, he feared that Kully had turned up on his doorstep and opened her heart out to him or maybe his brother was in need of his help, he had always said that he could call on him anytime and he would be there for him.

'Bruv, you okay, what's up?' Manjit asked with a concerned look on his face.

'Sorry to call you so late, but I just wanted know what time to pick you up for the Liverpool game tomorrow?' The only caveat being that they had to leave early the next morning in order to make the long trek up the motorway to the ground.

'Yeah, yeah that is cool, come to mine about 10 ish and I will be ready' Manjit said, he sounded sullen and deeply depressed and not the normal reaction that Hardeep had expected when they first talked about the prospect of watching the match. 'What's up, you sound well mashed?' Hardeep asked him.

'Bruv, have you not heard but I had a bust up with Kully and, well she has stormed out. I think she has gone to her parents.'

'Serious that is shit...what about?' Hardeep was asking him the one toe curling and cringe worthy question that he had being trying to avoid as soon as he opened his mouth to tell him. 'Err, nothing major, just usual couple stuff. It will probably blow over, yeah.' Manjit started to cry again as the pain of betrayal consumed him once again with the effects of the Bacardi now slowly taking firm residence within his body and distorting and twisting his emotional state.

Hardeep paused as he assessed his brother's mental state 'do you want me to come over? I will take the car, and I will be there in 5 minutes. We can talk because I am feeling like you bro.' Manjit wiped tear from his cheeks with his sleeve as he asked 'what do you mean?' Hardeep sat back on his chair in the study as he explained 'me and the missus have been on the rocks for ages. She has been staying at her parent's house. She has gone crazy over the last few days and to be honest I think she has been having an affair.' His words stabbed at Manjit's heart.

His mind suddenly flashed back to the times when he had ravaged his brother's wife in a variety of positions and not forgetting all manner of locations.

At the time oblivious to the heartache that was baked right in from the start. He snapped out of these thoughts as Hardeep's outpouring carried on 'I have suspected her for ages now, but proving it has been hard. How could she do it to me? I love her bruv, you understand and I if I ever caught the bhanchod then I would fucking kill him...I will let nobody take her from me.'

Manjit felt a tiny reprieve, as he was aware that his secret was safe and that the bunny boiler hadn't wagged her tongue yet. 'Bruv, that's rough. Listen you get some kip too and we will hook up and chat in the morning.'

Manjit again reached for the tablets in the bottle and tipped some on the counter whilst holding the mobile pressed against his ear, his thoughts jumbled and convoluted from the confession he had heard from his bro. His head was still pounding and the combination of nipple/testicle pain still shooting to his brain and not assuaging matters. He lifted one pill, two pills, and three pills into his mouth. What was he doing? He had now taken many more than was toxically acceptable for his body as he continued talking into the phone. He heard a bleeping sound and pulled the phone from his ear for a moment, and noticed that it was a withheld number. He ignored it and spoke with his brother instead.

'I am feeling pretty low and am just gonna go downstairs and watch a bit of TV, read a couple of letters I got and then turn in for a bit. I am feeling so cheesed off with life now and I think we are in the same boat hey little bro.' Hardeep's words disguising his disappointment on how their evenings had subsequently turned out. 'I have got a bottle of wine that I am going to open. We were saving that for our wedding anniversary.' Hardeep sobbed quietly to himself. Manjit vicariously felt his anguish and croaked 'see you tomorrow.' He put the phone down and stumbled back onto the kitchen seat with the mobile still firmly wedged in his hand. His head dizzy, the room spinning and his eyes blurring over by the minute. The pills were taking their toll; the sting in the tail was around the corner...

Chapter 22

—m—

Stranger

The phone rang again and without a skip of the heart-beat he placed the phone up to his ear.

'You're a dead man, you hear me. I am gonna mess you up, saala. You hurt my sister. I TOLD YOU BEFORE I WOULD KILL YOU!' The menacing screams of Joe were met by stunned debilitation and obedient silence. 'You hear me? You think you can cheat on her and laugh at my family? Nah I tell you what, you are dead, you are gonna suffer like you have made her suffer.' Manjit listened in sheer terror as the bile laced words flew freely from Joe's mouth.

His perspicuous threats scaring the living tutti out of Manjit as his life continued to crumble to ash around him. His eyes searched the kitchen for answers, the floor, the ceiling, anywhere, somehow he wished he could free himself from the menacing and life extinguishing situation he was now facing. The answers stared back at him from across the kitchen. BANG! The phone line went dead as Manjit tossed it on the table. He raced over to the bottle of Bacardi and quickly back to the table with the nectar of everlasting life very much gripped in his hand. He unscrewed the cap tossing it to the floor as he tilted his head back glugging the contents down his throat. The bottle had been three quarters full and within the next 15 seconds, in between a short gasp for air, he had expertly whittled it down to a quarter full and was still going strong.

Another few seconds later, he slammed the bottle histrionically on the kitchen table. It stared back at him, flashing, striped, spotted, large, small and very empty. His eyes played more tricks on him. He felt a twinge in his heart, in his bodily organs as they fought valiantly to combat the sudden intrusion of such a vast amount of damaging liquid. The phone rang again and he moved his head slowly to stare down at it. His reactions heavily impaired through the fusion of drink and drugs.

He laughed like a madman. The phone rang and vibrated more, teasing him to pick it up. Who could it be now he thought? His mind like a jumbled jigsaw. He stooped down and picked it up 'yeah.'

'How could you do that to my friend? You low life piece of scum! You guys are all the same, you bastard.' It was Rita phoning from her mobile. Kully had phoned her and had been crying on her shoulder once she had confessed to her parents and Joe about her broken marriage. Kully had asked Rita to promise that she would not phone and she had agreed.

It was only a short while later when Rita had spoken to Amar about the situation and the feelings of her own husband doing the same with her had she developed such a powerful necessity and compulsion to call him and give him a piece of her mind. Manjit listened and due to his state of mind and the eruption of sensations in his body laughed mockingly at Rita that only caused to inflame her feelings. 'Don't laugh about it, all you guys are the same. Just can't help yourself, one sniff of a bit of action and you just can't resist. You all make me sick, look at you, you don't even care do you?

Manjit was sobbing hard with intermittent laughs of pain as the grip of the phone weakened in his hand. It felt as though his heart was going to explode out of his shirt and pebbledash around the kitchen walls; equally, his liver threatened to rip open inside him and consume him from within.

'I am telling you stop laughing or I will come over there and shut your mouth for you.' Manjit chortled like a lunatic, hysterically falling to the floor. He didn't mean to, but it was his body's natural reflex action to his mental state. He then suddenly fell to the floor on his knees. He started wheezing, his free hand clutching his chest.

Rita screamed 'I am going to kill you piece of shit...' Amar suddenly grabbed the phone off of her and tried to calm her down. She stormed out of Amar's house.

Amar turned the phone off and threw it down as he chased after Rita. She had a focussed and determined look on her face, and wherever she was off to, she looked consumed and enchanted with a fury that he had never witnessed to date.

Manjit slowly regained his footing off the floor. He held his midriff with both hands, the phone still grasped and held in place on his chest by his hands. He slowly ambled over to the kitchen top where the pills were, he scooped a handful of them in his hand and staggered out into the hallway bouncing off the kitchen walls as he did so. He leant against the kitchen door frame, his mind desperately searching for the answers to how his life had turned into such a disaster. He was becoming a sure fire candidate for crystal meth abuse that much was for sure.

The problems were stacking up against him without respite as his life spiralled out of control; the imminent divorce, the people baying for his blood and the crazed stalker who had given him HIV. He knew there was every possibility of contracting full blown AIDS without proper medical attention, and this scared him to his core.

All these worries were becoming increasingly insurmountable as he threw several more pills into his mouth to numb the pain and take away the awful memories of the cesspit his life had become. The pills he was taking were the most powerful pain killers legally prescribed by doctors. They had been used last year when Kully had suffered a broken bone in a freak accident when she slipped on ice outside her house. Her bone had snapped in two places and Kully had pleaded with her doctor to prescribe her the strongest pain killers he had to assist her in sleeping at night. Manjit was not compus mentis and was sorrowfully unaware of these important factors, as the tablets had been consumed like pieces of candy throughout the last hour or so.

Manjit's heart again twitched and the pain seemed to sear through his left arm. He staggered some more and towards the front door, opening it and letting the evening air hit him. He fumbled in his pocket whilst still clutching his heart and brought out his wallet. He flicked it open with one hand and pulled out a small photo that he had always kept close to him. It was a photo of Kully hugging him in a trip to the Lake District when they had just got married. Manjit gently stroked her face with his thumb, his face scrunching up in pain as his heart twinged again, a sharp and knife edged pain. He winced and dropped the photo and his phone to the floor.

Suddenly, he sunk to his knees and then flopped over to one side, both hands now tightly clamping his chest. He then felt a tremendous weight on his chest, that of an elephant sitting on him, the wheels a Range Rover landing squarely on him. He gasped for breath, his eyes widened as the pain and sheer weight sunk in even deeper. The situation was critical, he was too young to die, this and many other pleading thoughts flickered across his mind.

His eyes rolled down to the floor as he laid there, the beautiful smile of Kully looking back at him through tear soaked and desperate eyes. He could do nothing as he felt his life oozing out of him; the realisation that he had suffered a massive heart attack had hit him straight between the eyes. He tried to reach for the photo again but his arm refused to work, he was paralysed and dying, he had gone this far in life only to be chewed up and spat out in such an unceremonious manner.

The sound of a car shuddering to a halt was heard outside, the slamming of a car door and the frantic footsteps scampering up the front garden path were mildly edifying for his soul. Manjit tilted his head up slowly to see who his rescuer was, the person who was going to snatch him back from the very depths of his nadir with such impeccable timing. The footsteps slowed down as the visitor slowly walked into the house standing a few feet away from his battered frame. Their face was obscured from the darkness of the hallway and the silhouette cast an imposing figure in the doorway with the street light behind them.

'Help me, please help me, call Hardeep please...' Manjit croaked in desperation. His hand was slowly inching towards the phone that was lying teasingly just out of his reach. He was almost there as his fingers slowly walked closer and closer to it, the Yellow Pages team on standby outside to snap him up for their next advert. The visitor however just stood there surveying the scene, their breathing rapid and skittish. Hands clenched with furious anger and lips pursed.

Manjit looked up again, he showed no emotion as he studied the strangers face, his heart and chest crushed again, this time the weight of a jumbo jet landing on it. He screamed like a distressed monkey and made one last desperate lunge for the phone. 'Pleaseeee...get me some help...I don't want to die.' His dying declaration had worked as the visitor walked forward and knelt down. The help had arrived and the ambulance was a mere phone call away.

Manjit braced himself and fought hard against the pain, he only had to last a few more minutes and then he would be in the hands of the paramedics, this small crumb of comfort kept him going, kept him strong and more importantly alive.

The visitor then slowly loosened Manjit's grip on the phone as Manjit watched through concentrated pain. Once loosened the visitor gently nudged the phone out of his hand and pushed it a few inches to one side and out of the dying victims reach. Manjit raised his head momentarily in utter shock and realisation that this was the end of the road. The face of evil stared back at him through the cloak of darkness, the dark shade of the night obscuring half their face with the street lights and moonlight combining to shine across the other half of the face. The fusion of good versus evil looking down on Manjit, as he took his last coughing and spluttering breath. The killer had arrived but their job was in the throes of being completed. The self inflicted death looming on the horizon. The death rattle moments away.

Suddenly the frowning face of the intruder looked down as Manjit slowly closed his eyes and slipped to his icy defeat. He died right there, his dreams, hopes and ambitions were all crushed in a whim. His life meaningless and his soul restless, his lifeless shell lay there prostrate. Manjit had rolled the dice of chance and lost bitterly. The Grim Reapers stamp had been embossed on his life and he was gone from this lifetime. The visitor sat in deep thought for a second before getting up and running out of the door in sheer panic. They had wanted him dead, but this was not the scene they had expected when they had arrived that evening... The stranger, intruder, visitor, whatever they were, now had Manjit's blood on their hands albeit just through their inaction, but who was this heartless soul?

—m—

Pensive

The next morning the alarm on Hardeep's mobile sounded causing him to shoot up in bed startled and with a swirling feeling of helplessness in his body, the sort of feeling that two twins would experience, a vicarious feeling of anguish that he could not put his finger on. Somehow, he knew his brother was hurt and he could hear his faint voice calling and reaching out for him, albeit this was now a fait accompli. He sidled out of bed sinking his bunion riddled feet into a pair of Donald Duck slippers and walked downstairs into the kitchen.

The time 9am and the Sunday morning dew shining through the window. He had half an hour or so to get ready before picking up his brother for the football game in Liverpool. He sat down and slumped his hands down on the table in front of him. He wiped his face with his hands and stared red eyed at the table. He felt terrible, the heavy drinking the night before and previous night had taken their toll on his system. His mind was elsewhere as his mind churned back over the nightmarish thought of his brother being in peril. His face scrunched up for a moment and then he decided the best way to find out would be to get over to his house right away and see for himself. Therefore, he skipped breakfast and began to get ready, shaving and showering like Speedy Gonzales on acid.

Half an hour later he was in his car, tickets in his pocket and primed to get into the day. He studied himself for a second in the rear view mirror, tilting it down to take a better look. His eyes were red with racoon type circles underneath, his skin puffy and blotchy and mouth like a rotting corpse. He stuck a chewing gum in his mouth and set off on the short journey to his brother's house. The sick feeling of apprehension and perception continuing to boil inside him.

Several minutes later, his car entered his brother's road. He pulled up outside and immediately noticed that the front door was indeed open, only slightly. He got out of the car and walked slowly up the path to investigate. He knew something was wrong, call it brotherly instinct, call it what you want, but he sensed that his brother's cries for help in his subconscious mind were tangible as he slowly push opened the door with his hand. He was moments away from the sick truth dawning on him, the realisation that his brother had taken his own life, albeit unwittingly and through an unfortunate sequence of events tipped by virtue of losing his wife and the pernicious thought of HIV gravely ruining his life forever.

The door creaked open and there he lay, motionless, in a scrambled heap on the floor, eyes closed and gone from the fulfilling and virtuous life he once used to lead. Hardeep stood there eyes open wide trying hopelessly to take in what he was seeing, his mind registering painfully that his brothers cries for help were real and that he was too late to save him, he was dead.

Hardeep knew this was so, they say you can smell death and a man with his experience of life was no different. He shook his head as tears streamed down his cheeks. His little brother had been snatched away from him. There was nothing more he could do as he crouched down and leaned back against the door frame. He felt nauseous as he fiddled in his pocket taking out his mobile phone where he dialled for an ambulance; it was a token call, as he knew what was obvious as Manjit's cold and lifeless body sat hauntingly across from him. Their bond had been insurmountable and now it was over, he would never be in his life again and the reality was too painful for him.

Several minutes later the sound of the two tones and flashing of the blue sirens of the ambulance came whirring down his road, and before he knew it the paramedics were standing over him and treating him for shock, whilst taking care of the rigor mortis that had set in on Manjit's body. The sick smell of death causing Hardeep to retch violently on to the shoes of the first paramedic when Manjit's body was moved to see if there was any need to administer first aid. The smell equivalent to steak and kidney pie wafting up to his nose like a Bisto advert and making him retch once again, this time over himself as he sat there a broken man.

Hardeep sobbed hard and in a sudden paroxysm screamed like a banshee letting out all of his anger. He was helped to his feet and was led to the rear of the ambulance where the sick covered guardian angel treated him for his condition. He lay on the stretcher bed in the rear with the tears from his eyes forming little pools on either side of him and soaking the fabric his weary body was laying on.

The paramedics meanwhile took the necessary arrangements to inform the relevant authorities to investigate whilst Hardeep slowly closed his eyes, his head full of remorse and debilitating thoughts of what could have been. Nothing was making sense to him as he drifted off to a deep and painful sleep.

Meanwhile over at Kully's parent's house, she sat there at the breakfast table slowly chewing on her bowl of cornflakes, musing the previous evening's events. She felt empty and beaten, her eyes lost in a haze of outrage and contemplation. What had she done? The severity of her actions would hold life long ramifications. At that moment, Joe walked in through the back door and looked startled when he saw his sister. His hair looked dishevelled and as though he had been dragged through a hedge backwards. His body was stout like that of a bull dog and he had a physique that would make any boxer proud. He stared at Kully for a moment before shutting the rear door. The door that led to the garden, down the side alleyway and out into the road.

His brown snake eyes not giving anything incriminating away as he tried to avoid any awkward questioning. Kully looked down at her bowl nervously. She was naturally not a morning person but with her fragile mental condition, she thought better than to engage in conversation other than offer her brother a token conversational pleasantry. 'You been out all night?' Joe had made it to the door leading out to the hallway and was stopped in his tracks by her rug pulling probe 'yeah I stayed out at…Arun's house.'

He looked sheepish and kept looking away from Kully's gaze occasionally shifting his eyes at her to assess her response. She looked surprised and equally guilt ridden 'I went out looking for you last night when you didn't come home.' Joe's furious reaction the previous evening had prompted her bloodhound search. She continued 'I also phoned your friends including Arun; he said you were not there.' Her words hung in the air with the spectre of doubt slowly seeping through the kitchen walls and around his muscular neck. There was a silence as he composed his response. He scratched his head and walked out talking over his shoulder 'I went there afterwards, I needed time to cool down.' He stormed off clearly fed up with the line of questioning and hint of accusation being levied at his door.

He ran upstairs and quickly took his clothes off, and dived into the shower, he was tired and his mind was a convoluted mess. It was obvious from everything that had been said and done that he had visited Manjit that evening. He washed his face and leaned back against the wall of the shower as the droplets of water cascaded down on his body. It was only a matter of time before the net closed in on him. He looked around; it seemed as though the walls of the shower had already begun to close in on him such was his sickening twinge of guilt.

Back at the hospital Hardeep opened his eyes and looked up at the ceiling as he tried to figure out where he was. He gently sat up and saw doctors and nurses milling around frantically tending to the walking wounded at the local hospital's accident and emergency section. He had been placed in a room next to the busy department with the reception nurse catching his eye and walking towards him with a clipboard in her hand. 'Mr Dhaliwal. How are you feeling?' The elderly nurse asked him.

He sat up some more, shifted his legs over the side of the table, and dangled them off the bed that he was on as he sat up erect. His face was concerned and anxious 'how long have I been here? Where is my brother?' His eyes looked around the ward, there was no sign of Manjit. At this precise moment a young black doctor walked beside the nurse and took hold of the clipboard 'leave this to me.' He ushered the nurse away and took the horse by the reins closing the curtain behind him and sitting on the bed alongside Hardeep.

He then proceeded to explain to Hardeep that his brother had died the previous evening from a deadly combination of pills, drink, and a freak heart attack, which was caused directly because of the lethal overdose he had consumed. The doctor reached out and placed his hand on his shoulder squeezing down hard. He was the purveyor of earth shattering news. Hardeep sat there pensive. Hardeep looked down at his own hands and shook his head for a second. He had evil thoughts of revenge circulating in his head, and he knew what he had to do. Any wisps of happiness in his life had been eroded, eradicated for good.

The doctor then went on to explain that he had received the official report and it was clear that he had died from a self inflicted overdose. The next 10 minutes then involved a discussion about the morgue, further next of kin details and funeral arrangements via an undertaker. The doctor explained that he had informed his brother's next of kin, his wife Kully.

Hardeep immediately asked how she had taken the news knowing that they had split that evening. The doctor affirmed that her reaction was like that of any grieving widow, shock, anger and devastation. Hardeep looked away searching for some answers from some-where. The doctor probed further asking him if he wanted to inform his wife of what had happened, as she would be worried.

Upon hearing this Hardeep stood up and grabbed the doctor by the lapels running with him and thrusting him against the connecting curtain. Both of them spilling over into the adjacent section and toppling over an elderly female patient who was lying in her bed peacefully performing a number two in her bed bowl after having had her piles removed in a painful operation. Her look of sheer terror was all too real as the pair of them somersaulted over the bed yanking her with them as she skidded across the shiny hospital floor.

The doctor and Hardeep remained locked together landing with an incredibly gut twisting thud on the other side of the bed, the contents of the elderly patients piss bowl tipping over their faces and covering them with warm frothy piss and faeces. The female patient meanwhile continued skidding and defecating as she did so along the ward floor leaving a long and slimy trail of brown tutti in a strange zig zag shape. She stopped skidding when she smashed through the emergency doors and landed head first into large floor standing pot plants that then toppled on top of her head. She looked back at them, out of breath and with evil eyes peering through the plants leaves. Her arse was red like a baboon and with a smattering of brown adding to the embarrassment and her misery.

Hardeep stood the doctor up apologising profusely about his misguided reaction to his wife's name. He tried to explain how her very name invoked feelings of rage within him from her leaving him. The doctor moved away from him displeased and with a mixture of yellow and brown froth dripping down into his mouth. Within seconds security were called, who duly led Hardeep out turfing him out into the street with stern warnings and threats.

This was his cue to discharge himself. He then made his way back to his parent's house where he sobbed like a baby in the arms of his mum and dad (Santosh and Balwant). The family wept tears for India and set about with visits to the hospital and undertakers along with necessary but yet painful calls to their nearest and dearest relatives. This was indeed a sorrowful and heart-breaking period for everyone, none more so than Hardeep, who at this moment felt like he had lost everything in one foul swoop. He was truly caught in the grip of an earthquake.

Over the next few days, the condolences poured in from every corner of the globe such was the popularity of Manjit with his effervescent spirit and unbridled chutzpah. His spirit leaving an indelible mark on each and every person that he had ever come into contact with, none more so than his brother. Tej and Saty were devastated and both broke down in the most harrowing manner. Rita's reaction was indifferent and she showed no emotion but rather said that she would phone Kully and help her friend get over this ordeal. Hardeep moved on to the next friend and family members on the list, he was focussed on his mission.

Hardeep spent the entire week at his parent's house and did not return home not even once such was his duty to provide a steely rock like framework for his parents; it was not every day that they would lose their son. It has been said that there is no grief worse than a parent seeing the dead body of their child, and within Asian circles this was the lowest that anyone could ever have felt. With these thoughts in his mind, Hardeep stayed close by, even eschewing his sleep on many occasions and making funeral arrangements and calls to guests worldwide sometimes through the night. His parents appreciated their sons support during these turbulent and harrowing times.

During the week, Hardeep decided that he would also tell Raj who had been staying at her parent's house for the last few days in case she had not heard from the others. She picked up the phone right away and responded similar to Rita. She did not sound too upset or worried and came back at him with a cold and calculating response 'well that is life, and that is what happens when you...' She stopped mid sentence and instead thought best than to finish off what she was about to say.

Hardeep did not even attempt to embroil himself in a distasteful and meaningless argument with her and dismissed her apathetic attitude with a pinch of salt. He simply terminated the call and knew that she would keep for another day. That much he knew...

CHAPTER 24

—⁂—

Dirges in the night

A whole week had now passed and it was the day of the funeral – Friday morning.

The crematorium had been booked. This was the chosen method for Sikhs to send their loved ones on to the next level. The undertakers, a local firm that Hardeep had arranged *Desi to Ashes and Co* had brought the coffin around to the house in the morning with all the family, friends and other close associates standing around the coffin as it was gently placed in the middle of the living room. All the guys were dressed in black, whilst the women wore white Asian suits. Both colours representing the subdued colours of mourning, when a loved one passes in Asian traditions.

The head was by the bay windows at Hardeep's parent's home in Greenford, with Manjit's feet facing away from the windows. It was considered bad luck for the bed's in the house to be arranged in such a way that you slept with your feet away from the window's as it resembled the way that you would lay in your coffin as was the case here today.

The coffin lid was lifted up by the undertakers and there laid the beautifully embalmed and radiant face of Manjit. He looked peaceful as though in a deep slumber, his hands resting gently on top of his body and lips subtly arranged as though he was smiling. His body had been cleaned as per tradition the night before and he had been suitably dressed in a chosen ensemble by his crest fallen dad and other uncle's. The devastating and demoralising feeling of having to cremate your son was consuming and gnawing away at their souls. The cleansing ritual was performed at the undertaker's mortuary where the guys had been quietly chanting religious hymns and crying whilst performing the task in hand. The body had been embalmed to preserve the skin and prevent the flesh and carcass from decaying before it was displayed at home.

The opening of the lid brought on huge banshee like wailing from the family with genuine cries of loss and anguish from his mum and aunties along with quiet sobs from Balwant and other family members. This was generally frowned upon as the public showing of grief or 'antam sanskar' was frowned upon in Sikh funeral traditions.

The religious chanting of *wahe guru, wahe guru* and other such *shabads (hymns)* were reverberating around the room, and filling the air with an unfathomable feeling of injustice and desolation. Suddenly 85 year old auntie Chagvinder dramatically spun on a six pence and fainted in the most histrionic fashion as she stood glaring beady eyed from the other side of the room, the emotions overcoming her as she fell. She belly flopped to the floor face first, letting out the sound of a harpooned whale, with her dentures sliding across the floor to the sound of open mouthed gasps from the audience.

The surrounding family quickly placed her in the recovery position and attempted to resuscitate her with gentle slaps to her face. This worked as she swiftly regained her composure and began sucking her gums obviously looking for her missing dentures. Balwant wiped the dentures on the side of his trousers and quickly placed them back in her mouth. She looked up thankfully, as her weary shock ridden frame was placed on a nearby seat and stunned the mourners as she moved her mouth up and down like Dracula.

Balwant had popped them back in her mouth upside down and thus ensued the comedy act on such a serious occasion.

Once the commotion had passed and with the dentures finally inserted the correct way, she sat quietly sipping on a glass of water provided to her from another auntie, the funeral ritual continued.

One by one the mourners walked around the coffin and either placed there hand on the lifeless body of the prodigal son to pay their respects, kissed his forehead or placed money on the coffin. The crying and emotions spilling over in nigh on every case, the suffering, distress and misery palpable through every mourner's moment of heart wrenching respect.

Hardeep was standing to the far right of the coffin, his black sunglasses concealing the sheer devastation and disappointment in his eyes, a feeling that he could and should have somehow done more to save his brother. If only he had gone around and talked to him that evening then things may have been different. He questioned his brother's state of mind for him to have been so low, so helpless that he was compelled to take his own life in such a manner. It was all too much and he felt the guilt like a sword though his heart. He looked up and around the room, behind the glasses and in the darkest depths of his mind he had one word echoing with malevolence – VENGANCE!

Standing next to him and looking shell shocked was Raj. Her body seemingly shaking from seeing her former lover lying there as dead as a doorknob and any possible future she had mapped out in her warped mind smashed to smithereens. Her eyes never left his face as she struggled to keep her hands from shaking out of control and conveying the guilty emotion that her body was riddled with at that moment.

He could see Amar and Rita standing next to each other over to the left corner of the coffin. Amar was impassive as was to be expected. He never knew Manjit and therefore had no connection with him whatsoever. Rita meanwhile looked around with a strange and wild glint in her eyes. He had never seen this before. They say that grief taps in to emotions never previously seen before, character traits that have been dormant for years upon years until such a sorrowful occasion brings them to the fore.

Hardeep studied her for a moment as she shifted her eyes from side to side, a guilty glaze painted across her face. This look confused Hardeep and made him feel decidedly uncomfortable. Her eyes suddenly caught Hardeep's and she hastily shifted her eyes back to the floor as if staring at her own clogs, deeply unsettling and suspicious he thought to himself as if she was concealing something.

Hardeep then looked across at his mum and dad, they were both propping one another up, pillars of strength and fortitude and trying to send their darling

beta on to the next world with the dignity and peace
that he would have wanted. As proud Sikhs, they were
truly devastated but equally had accepted that it was
Gods *'hukam' (wish)* that he had taken their son. It
seemed that it was his time. They had accepted that.
However for Hardeep, it was different and his loss was
too much for him to bear as he felt the water dams burst
and floods of over sized and soggy tears came shuttling
down his face and dripping unforgiving down the black
jacket of his suit.

Kully and Joe were also nearby, both of them had
been looking straight ahead and unaware that Hardeep
had locked his gaze on them. Joe's face was concentrated
and earnest. He glanced sideward's at Hardeep and gave
him a hard stare before looking straight ahead.

He looked an angry young man and it was clear that
he despised both Manjit and Hardeep for the mere fact
that they were associated through brotherhood. He was
there for his sister and nothing else. He was there to fend
off the sickening and unjust accusations that he felt were
going to be levied at his sister's door for walking out on
her husband and causing his untimely death. He was
there for this insurance and this alone, hence the glare at
Hardeep as if to warn him away, the look was obvious
and registered immediately with Hardeep, the fight and
any hostility towards Kully or even Joe being sucked out
of him instantaneously.

Meanwhile Tej and Saty were languishing and shim-
mering towards the back of the room and behind the
hordes of mourners. Rita turned her head around,
caught the eye of Tej, and gave her an acknowledging
look before looking back again. She was sweating, but
the humidity within the room had been cranked up a few

notches with the amount of people cramming into the grief filled arena.

The marital problems experienced by Saty and Tej had been put to one side during this period of mourning and more importantly Saty had been brought up to speed with the crucial confession made by Raj that fateful evening last week with her outburst at the girls evening.

He had already concluded that this scarlet woman was the one that his fallen friend had been having an affair with and somehow was linked to his death, but at this moment he had no proof. With these churned up thoughts rattling around in his mind, he glared at his new found nemesis from across the room.

Meanwhile Kully made a passing perusal with her eyes around the room, and at that precise moment Raj was doing the same. Their eyes met and the two warriors locked gazes staring iniquitously into the white's of one another's eyes. There was no love lost as they held the gaze for a few seconds and then both concomitantly looked away, the erstwhile friendship tempered now with feelings of hate, jealousy and betrayal.

The undertakers who had stood by patiently with backs against the wall so as not to interfere with such an occasion now moved forward beckoned by Balwant. They gently lifted the lid of the coffin and began to replace it as the mourners started to move out through the front door and into their respective cars to make their way down to the crematorium for the final farewell. As this was happening and the *wahe guru, wahe guru* chants continued, Gaurav who had kept a deliberately low profile standing towards the back of the hordes of mourners slowly made his way to the front and hugged Hardeep tightly. It was a strong and reassuring gesture of brotherly emotion that almost made Hardeep's knees buckle as he gripped his dear friend...

They embraced and cried hard letting the emotions pour out unashamedly. Tears soaking the shoulders of their suits 'he loved you man, you know he always told me you were everything to him.' Gaurav's words inadvertently slicing the gaping wound even wider as Hardeep took his sunglasses off for a moment and screamed loudly causing the slowly departing mourners to jolt and look back in abject horror. Gaurav squeezed his friend tight to him again and whispered soothing words of comfort 'be strong, everyone is looking at you now, keep your chin up. You have to get through this day, okay. I am here for you.'

Hardeep let go of his dear friend and nodded his head understanding and feeling the kind sentiments on this black day in the life of his family. Amar never looked up at Gaurav once. He was mindful and respectful that this was not the place to goad him with a look of any description, as he knew that such occasions and emotional states had the capacity to transmogrify folk into hell bent animals. That was a scene that he did not wish to exploit.

His military mission brief was to ensure that he provided a rock like shoulder for his girlfriend even though she still had not told him exactly where she had disappeared to for an hour on the evening that Manjit had died.

The coffin was slowly carried outside by the undertakers and placed in the hearse ready to be driven to the crematorium. The mourners were all settling in their cars and waiting for the hearse to drive off slowly down the road when Hardeep walked past Rita and Tej as they were engaged in conversation.

'I had no idea that Kully and Manjit were having problems in their marriage. They seemed the perfect couple, I am so in shock and will miss him so much.' Tej's voice began to crack as the emotion cut through. Rita looked at her and could not resist the snake like comment that came out of her mouth 'yeah looks like all couples have secrets don't they...hey Tej?'

Her face scowling as she spoke. A hidden under current was present in her tone and a look that caused Tej to take a step back. 'What do you mean by that?' This was hardly the time and place to engage in matters of such insignificance but the blue paper was slowly burning now and there was no turning back.

'Look don't play innocent with me I saw you the other day with that guy.' She suddenly let rip with her accusation cutting and hurtful.

'What guy?' Tej continued to be defiant and looked genuinely confused for someone who was used to the slippery road of cheating and lying on a day to day basis with her husband.

Rita laughed knowingly as she went for the coup de gras 'the man I saw at your house on Friday morning, when you popped your head outside the door all sheep-ishly. The day when Saty was out, remember now?' That was it she had caught her out. The damning evidence was there on a plate. Tej scrunched her face up as her mind began to do cartwheels. She thought back and then delivered her succinct response 'thanks for choosing your moment to ask me that. However, if it is any of your business Saty and me have been having marriage problems and the guy you are talking about was a marriage councillor. His name is *Anil,* you want to call him to for your investigation?' Her sarcasm suitably cutting. 'I had invited him to my house on that day to help us sort out our issues...satisfied or do you want more?'

Tej was losing her temper and for a second raised her voice with sheer disappointment of Rita's accusing and condemning tone. Rita looked appalled as the reality of her faux pas slowly dawned on her 'and Saty?' she asked.

'Oh don't worry, he was inside. Our car has been at the mechanic's with a radiator problem. It was the only way I could get him to see a councillor.' Rita immediately felt the sickening feeling of guilt twisting her innards and went to apologise to her friend, but Tej moved her body back. 'I thought you knew me better than that, leave me alone.' She walked past her brushing her shoulder as she did so and made her way to her parked car; her disappointment visible and the full force felt head on like a tonne of bricks by a startled Rita.

Hardeep went to sit in the undertaker's second car. This was the car that had been booked primarily for the close family members. He looked up and through his sunglasses noticed that Raj was standing by herself over on the corner of the street. He could see that she was desperately dragging on a cigarette. Strange he thought to himself but he had never seen her smoke once during their marriage. He noticed that she was looking anxious and worried but again realised that everone had their own idiosyncrasies and that the human body reacted differently for individuals in times of trauma such as these.

All folk made their way to the crematorium and the coffin was sent to the smouldering furnaces below to the sounds of mourners continually chanting *wahe guru wahe guru*. The crematorium room packed to the rafters with people from all over the globe such was his popularity. Whilst this was all going on Raj who seemed a little more relaxed managed to slip out the rear of the room undetected and shuffled about in her pocket, she took out another cigarette and lighter and sparked up. She stood alone in the car park, next to a waste bin and scanned the surrounding vicinity for other people. It was baron and desolate just like her heart and soul.

She took a long drag from the cigarette as ash from the tip curled up and fell to the floor. It was then that she began to rummage around in her pocket, where she produced a folded piece of paper. She looked around again, the car park remained soulless. She drew the cigarette from her mouth, tossed it to one side, and watched it smouldering on the gravel staring back at her. She unfolded the letter and stared at the contents. It was the letter that she had received from the hospital regarding her test results for HIV. She smiled wryly and took out her lighter and holding it up against the bottom corner of the paper proceeded to set it alight.

She watched the fire crackling and smoke bellowing past her face. Her eyes, a picture of pure evil and intent. It was done; her mission had been accomplished as she had meticulously planned. If she could not have him then no-one else would. The pain would have been unbearable. They simply did not come any more evil than this specimen did as she held the paper gingerly by her fingertips watching it smoulder to nothing. 'Sucker!' She slyly mumbled to herself before tossing the last remaining fiery paper into the waste basket.

The HIV had been a mere point scoring rouse to hurt him like he had hurt her, to inflict some long term mental damage to him for turning his back on her at the height of their stormy affair. It had worked, as the guilt of the

HIV had been an inexorable link to Manjit's fragile state of mind causing him to search for answers in alcohol and pills, leading to his ultimate defeat. Her exhilarating Oscar winning performance had hoodwinked him emphatically to the point of no return.

This was her perverse way of driving the final nail in his coffin and concluding this chapter of infidelity.

She had planned it this way from the moment he had shunned her with that phone call from the office. Her seething determination to seek and mete out her own personal style of revenge had ultimately ended in the taking of his life. It seemed that her evil intentions had even extended to her watching him die before her very eyes that fateful day.

Now it was over and she turned to face the crematorium building as the smoke from the furnaces below bellowed out through the brick built chimneys situated in the distance towering above her head. She smirked sadistically and dusted her hands, this chapter was now in the past, and it was time to move on. She flipped open her phone as the mourners started to slowly walk out of the building as they stared up at the chimney.

She pressed several buttons as she composed a text message before flicking through the stored numbers on her phone stopping at her chosen target. By now all the mourners were outside and talking quietly to one another. She pressed send and looked up for the reaction. In amongst the crowd a mobile phone vibrated as the recipient took out their phone to inspect the message they had received;

'If you want I can come over tonight. I think I can help you to overcome this terrible day's events...Raj'

Gaurav looked up and searched the crowd of people finally spotting Raj standing a few feet away detached from the rest. He looked back down at his phone and text back;

'Sure…wear something nice…'

Saty had seen all the exchanging of text messages from where he was standing and his breath caught in his throat, as the reality of his suspicions began to unravel in front of him. He simply could not fathom how someone could have been so ruthless. The evil and murderous bitch he thought to himself. Raj was Manjit's mistress, the married one, that day when he had called after he had finished work, it was HER all along. It all made sense; she couldn't have him so she ensured that her arch enemy Kully couldn't keep him either. That would have been too much to bear under the circumstances, so she drove him to suicide instead.

Raj meanwhile noticed that Saty had seen her and smirked at him. It seemed as though the black widow had made another kill. Was her murderous and turbulent secret going to be taken to the grave with her? Her doll like façade a perfect ruse as another soon to be victim succumbed to her. He shook his head in disbelief as she had already moved on to her next prey without a shred of remorse. What was Gaurav's fate going to be he thought glumly?

All day she had been desperately trying to conceal the obvious expression on her face and to all intents and purposes, it had worked.

Saty with a heavy heart did not know how to broach the subject with Hardeep about the deceit that had been taking place under his friend's nose, and that his treacherous wife had been sleeping with his very own brother. He had already sat on this secret for over a week after Tej had told him, but was unsure up until the texting moment how to off load the rucksack of anguish to his dost (friend). Now he knew he had to tell Hardeep or the pain of letting her get away with it would consume him from within.

Meanwhile the mourners all gradually made their way back to the parent's house. Hardeep whispered to Balwant that he was going to go home for the first time in the entire week just to check if the house was okay and to have a little time by himself. His father understood and gave him a big and warm hug. The kind of hug that whiled away all the worries and lost they had suffered. Hardeep then went home and slowly walked up his path before shutting the door behind him. He pressed his body up against the door and cried some more pressing his forefinger and thumb of his left hand into his eyes trying in vain to stem the flow of tears. After a few minutes, he stopped and slowly looked up, his face suddenly full of pure disgust. An evil so pure and vile that even Lucifer himself would be cowering in trepidation. He too knew what had happened. Something was wrong, very wrong...

CHAPTER 25

———

Cogitating

Hardeep walked into the living room and took his jacket off throwing it onto the sofa. The room was dark and moody reflecting his state of mind and disturbed thoughts. The curtains still drawn shut from last week when he had sat by himself reading and relaxing whilst his brother had taken his own life nearby. He looked lost; his thoughts gnarled and deep rooted, his spirit and resolve that of a broken man as he slumped next to his jacket on the sofa loosening his tie. The sudden relief he found as he undid his shirt button was amazing, the tension seeming to pour out of his fingertips. He sat there replaying the events of the days prior to his brother's death and the sadness that followed.

The introspection of his own soul, the musing thoughts shuttling back and forth laced with the faintest signs of mockery. He never thought he would have the power or resoluteness to see this darkest of weeks through. The clutch of inescapable anguish had eroded his senses and destroyed his very being like the most malignant of cancers; the thought of losing his brother was outlandish and despicable. The peaks and troughs of life had all been witnessed by him within the last couple of weeks.

His eyes full of sorrow of hurt and insufferable loss scanned the room. Suddenly they stopped and settled on a half empty bottle of wine that was sitting neatly on some papers on the coffee table in the middle of the room. It was the wine that he had opened that fateful evening; the one he told his brother that he was going to consume before putting the phone down to him. He stared through the bottle with empty and heavy eyes, the skip of regret and desperate longing suddenly filling the room and shaking him to his core. What had caused his sudden apprehension and bemoaning?

He lifted his body, almost shearing his own body from the sofa like a velcro strip and reached out placing his hand around the throat of the bottle, gripping it as if he was choking the neck of a turkey. He then began to sob hysterically, hyperventilating and shaking his head. His shoulders continued to bounce up and down the more he recalled and yearned for his brother. He lifted the bottle off the papers and unscrewed the cap tossing it across the room with furious anger. It bounced off the walls and landed by the windows.

He looked down at the papers that lay there mockingly and rolled his head back whilst lifting the bottle of wine up and taking a hearty swig in an attempt to eradicate the pain that he was feeling. He looked at the papers again and tried to shut out the torment and self persecution he was suffering. He took another swig and then stood up screaming 'you bastards,' as he hurled the wine bottle against the living room wall. It smashed into a thousand pieces throwing shards of glass everywhere including back on to him, the remaining contents spilling over the sofa's and staining the walls and carpet.

He didn't care, his mind was in turmoil and he had temporarily lost control of all sensibility.

He sat back down slowly whilst surveying the damage that had been caused, his face a constant disturbed frown, his lips pointing downwards as though they were being pulled down by heavy weights.

He reached into his trouser pocket and after a few seconds of shuffling produced a pen. He twirled the pen slowly in between his fingers as he stared at the papers. They were now screaming for him to pick them up and put them out their misery. He stared some more before leaning forward and scooping them up in his hand and resting them on his lap. He looked down at the brown envelope that was nestling neatly between the white papers that he had picked up.

He looked up for a second as though searching for some inspiration; he rolled his eyes as he looked back down locking pen to paper. He started to write out the one name that had been on his mind for the past week, the day that his brother had died and the 3 months before his death, the woman he loved more than life itself, the woman he would die for, his wife Raj. He wrote her name out several times, each time the ink pressing deeper and firmer into the paper. Each time the wrath seeping through, they say the pen is mightier than the sword and this was very much the case in the dark and brooding cavern that was synonymously his mind and living room.

Suddenly his mobile phone ring tune played, the vibration heard though his jacket. He rummaged for the phone and raised it to his ear. He was not in the mood for conversational pleasantries and was met by a deathly silence.

He had not had the gumption or the foresight to check the caller Id, and therefore he was not sure who, or what was waiting for him on the other end of the phone.

The phone line then went dead. The caller had hung up leaving Hardeep slightly miffed. He placed the phone back by his side and looked back down at the paper. He drew a firm line through the name Raj, and again through her name where he had repeated it and continued to do so in a frenzy. The pen sweeping through angrily and with an untapped menace.

The phone rang again and he answered. It was Saty 'I have been trying to get through to you but I got cut off. I need to tell you something and fast.' The truth was about to be revealed to Hardeep especially as Saty had seen this conclusion being played out with sickening malice before his eyes. Hardeep terminated the call without further ado, and then switched the phone off completely. He had other things on his mind.

There was a reason why he had not returned home for a week since Manjit's death, a very good reason.

He took a deep breath and then flipped over the paperwork that rest on his lap and held them up teasingly towards his face. The letter address label read 'Karupa Sup Private Eye Agency. Underneath in another smaller envelope he slowly took out a photo of Raj walking out of a bed and breakfast followed by Manjit. He looked at the next photo and there was another photo again of the duplicitous lovers caught in flagrante delecto in a passionate embrace within the same bed and breakfast, before they slithered up the stairs to cover themselves in another lustful tryst.

Hardeep's eyes swelled up with hate as he violently scrunched the photo's up and let out a long painful sigh, his mind clearly trying desperately to cling on to a romanticised past. The dates on the photo's indicated that they had been taken approximately ten days ago, the very day that the lovers had in fact broken up, the same week that Raj had gone berserk inventing details of her alleged HIV scare and campaigning to win Manjit for good or eradicate him – FOR GOOD! The same week that Hardeep had been telling Manjit that he suspected that his wife was cheating, and the same week that Hardeep had arranged for the dropping off of the enveloped photographic evidence by Gurpreet when he was out at the Masala Beer Factory with the boys.

Hardeep had enlisted the assistance of the Karupa Sap Private Eye Agency a week prior to that, as he had become increasingly suspicious as to his wife's behaviour and reluctance to get physical with him. He had been on the phone to Gurpreet, one of the field operatives from the discreet Yellow Pages firm to seek out the results that he was paying so handsomely for.

He was praying that she would tell him that he had nothing to worry about and that his paranoia was not founded in truth, and his wife was not having an affair.

It had taken her a little while to develop the photo's due to technical problems with her equipment. The occasion that they were seen in the coffee shop together was when Gurpreet had offered a veiled hint that she had some evidence for him without elaborating in too much detail, not until she had fully investigated the circumstances that she had photographed herself through her own diligent enquiries.

On the Saturday outside in her car when they had been out drinking, she had delivered the brown envelope to Hardeep with the instructions that it was just a letter and that he was to open it at home. He had already told her that he was out drinking with his brother and she knew that a couple of Punjabi guys drinking would not be the ideal environment for such a revealing secret to be divulged, especially when she had subsequently discovered that the evidence actually incriminated his brother.

She reiterated that he was to open it later that evening whilst alone, and at home and that he would understand why this was the case.

Hardeep had acted obediently and later that evening after he had spoken with Manjit, he opened the bottle of wine and the brown envelope. It was at that very moment where his world collapsed around his feet. Further fuelled by drink from the wine bottle and vengeance, his anger had boiled over. He had lost that infamous temper that had been suppressed for so many years.

Jumping in his car, heavily intoxicated, and with the most evil intent he raced off in search of the Judas that swam in the very water's as he did, drank the same milk from his saucer and slept with his wife under his nose. His intention was to inflict maximum damage on his treacherous brother.

As Manjit died before him, he felt not a shred of remorse, instead gleefully looked deep into his eyes and into his soul as his brother pleaded for his life begging him to save him. That he could not do, not now!

Drunk and enshrouded with furious wrath he simply wanted to hurt Manjit for betraying him. He had broken the one sacred rule of any brethren - Never mess with your brother's wife!

No matter what the temptation is...

That night Hardeep had stood by as Manjit his dear brother paid for his indiscretion, his *'Naughty Indian Affair'* with his life. Now with his brother out of the way, his wife would love him again or she would be sorry too. He would then slowly be able to rekindle the *'masala'* in their marriage. That was ALL he had ever wanted, no matter who got in the way...

'Amantes sunt Amentes' - Lovers are Lunatics!

Lightning Source UK Ltd.
Milton Keynes UK
19 July 2010

157191UK00001B/71/P